KALEIDOSCOPE

KALEIDOSCOPE

BRIAN SELZNICK

SCHOLASTIC PRESS / NEW YORK

Library of Congress Cataloging-in-Publication Data available

ISBN 978-1-338-77724-6

10 9 8 7 6 5 4 3 2 1   21 22 23 24 25

Printed in China   62

First edition, September 2021

Book design by Brian Selznick and Charles Kreloff

For Cathy St. Germans

To fall in love is to make an appointment
with heartbreak.

—Matthew Lopez, *The Inheritance*

Everything changes, nothing ends.

—Ovid, *Metamorphosis*

KALEIDOSCOPE

"Go on," he said. "Look through it."

I picked up the kaleidoscope and held it to my eye.

"It's beautiful," I said.

As I turned the kaleidoscope, the mirrors and colored bits of glass rearranged and fractured the world.

"Now look at me," he said.

Part One

MORNING

.

A TRIP TO THE MOON

•

I looked out over the water and wondered if anything truly existed beyond the horizon. Reports of monsters beneath the waves and gods above the clouds had been around since the dawn of time, but I wanted to know for sure. So, on the morning of my thirteenth birthday, as the sky turned pink and gold, I stole a ship from my father's fleet and sailed with my friend James past the pillars of Hercules into the West Ocean. On the twelfth day of the voyage, a storm blew down from heaven, so fierce the water itself was lifted in a spout from the ocean, and our ship with it. James and I lashed ourselves to the masts with heavy ropes, closed our eyes, and prayed.

When we opened our eyes again, we were on the shore of an unknown land. A group of men appeared and took us through a dense jungle to a palace at the top of a great mountain. We were marched through long empty corridors, until we came upon a blue carpet that was thrown aside to reveal a door cut into the floor. A silver key was produced by one of the men and the door in the floor was opened, revealing a long downward staircase. James and I were brought to the bottom, where we stepped into the most wonderful crystal cavern. A sad-looking man was sitting on a throne made of gold.

"I am the King of the Moon," he said. "Who are you?"

"The *moon?*" I said in shock. "We are on the *moon?*"

"Of course you are on the moon," replied the King. "Where did you think you were?"

"The Earth!"

"Why would you be on the Earth?"

"It is where we live. It is where we came from."

"The Earth? Then how did you get up *here?*"

"It must have been the storm," I said.

"Well, you must have great powers," said the King. "You will help us win the battle."

"What battle?" asked James.

"*What battle?*" repeated the King, shocked. "The battle against the Sun!"

James got a familiar look on his face, and I knew he was not satisfied with this answer. "Why are you fighting with the Sun?" he asked. "You shine because of the reflected light of the Sun."

I smiled at James, whose vast learning was one of the reasons I wanted him by my side on this trip. His friendship and loyalty were the other reasons.

"The Sun is a Monster who believes there should *never* be darkness or night!" proclaimed the King of the

Moon. "Without darkness, there is no *night*, and without night, there is no *sleep*, and without sleep, there are no *dreams*." The King of the Moon stood and raised his fist to the sky. "And without dreams, everything dies."

The ground beneath our feet began to rumble.

"Ah," said the King of the Moon, "the spiders from Mars have arrived."

The battle raged for five hundred years. The spiders from Mars spun webs between the planets and we rode in our ship across the galaxy. The Soldiers of the Sun, made of light so bright it hurt to look at them, were relentless as the war raged on. The Men of the Moon were over-powered and many died bravely around us. As the blinding enemy advanced on us, we found ourselves unable to fight them directly, and we thought all was lost. But James saw our shadows cast against the sails of the ship, and he realized these shadows could fight when we could not. James's shadow was bravest of all, leading the charge. I watched in awe as it single-handedly drove back the Soldiers of the Sun, until peace was called and balance was restored.

The King of the Moon, exhausted from the fight, asked James to take his place on the throne of the Moon. James said yes, as I knew he would, and vowed to be a good king.

On the morning of his coronation, he grabbed my

hand, and without saying a word, we had an entire conversation.

    —Stay.
        —I can't. I don't belong here, but you do.
  —I'm not sure I can do this on my own.
      —I know you can.

He reached out his hand and I held it. I closed my
eyes so he wouldn't know the other thing I was thinking:
How am I going to live without you?

I boarded our ship and sailed back to Earth on a
cloud.

I wondered how much the world had changed
in the five hundred years I'd been gone . . . and was
utterly shocked when I saw my father, alive and well,
waiting for me at the dock when the ship returned. He
was angry I'd stolen one of his precious ships, and
he pulled me from the vessel and dragged me home,
where I was punished and sent to my room. Even though
I had been fighting among the stars for centuries, only a
few days had passed on Earth. No one believed my story,
and when James's mother came to me, weeping on her
knees, wanting to know where her son was, she found no
comfort in learning he'd become a king. Out of her mind

with grief, she told me James must have fallen overboard and drowned. She blamed me for his death.

I can still hear the sound of her cries as my father led her from my room. "Murderer!" she called. "Bring me back my son!"

But James could not come back. He was on his throne, making sure the universe was safe for dreaming.

THE GIANT

•

E very morning, I saw the boy sitting alone by the
St. Germans River. He had a favorite spot, on the
big rock under the old tree. I'd wanted to talk to him for
a long time, but I knew we were not allowed to speak to
humans. Mother had made that very clear. But I was
lonely and the boy looked lonely too. I'd never broken
any rules before. I always did what I was told. I brought
home food and listened to the elders in the caverns below
the hills. I learned how to walk without leaving footsteps,
and I knew how to become invisible by turning sideways,
just like Mother taught me. But still I was lonely.

Sometimes the boy brought food to eat when he was
sitting on the rock, and other times he just looked up
into the clouds. It was only on afternoons he fell asleep
that it felt safe enough for me to come closer. I watched
him from my sideways place across the river, and when
his eyes closed and he seemed to be dreaming, I stepped
across the water. He was no bigger than the end of my
finger. I thought about the eggs that sometimes fell from
nests and cracked open on the ground. The little wet
birds inside were not yet ready to live, and that's what the

boy looked like. He was so tiny and fragile, as if he too was not yet ready to live.

I wondered what he was dreaming about. Were his dreams like mine? Sometimes, I was lost in the vast dark caverns beneath the mountains. But mostly my dreams were filled with water and forests and strange animals and hot food. Sometimes I could fly. The sensation of being in the air with the birds and the clouds was so real that I often felt the crisp sky on my skin for minutes after I woke up. Even though they started out in eggs that could easily break, I still thought birds were lucky. I wished I was a bird.

"Who are you?" came a small voice from very far away.

The boy had woken up. I quickly turned sideways and became invisible to him. I stepped back across the river and watched as the boy propped himself up on his elbows. I didn't know what his words meant, but I could tell he was unafraid. I wondered if he thought I'd been a dream.

The next day, the boy brought an apple with him and set it down on the edge of the rock. The red dot was so small I could hardly see it, but somehow I knew it was meant for me. Remaining sideways, I stepped across the river and placed my finger at the edge of the rock. There was no way for me to pick up the apple, because it was too small, so I let the boy see me, just for a fraction of a second. The boy blinked and shivered, as if he'd gotten a chill. But he picked up the apple and placed it in the air. The moment it touched me, the apple became invisible too. I placed the apple on my tongue. I couldn't bite down on it since it was so small, but when it was crushed in the vastness of my mouth, I could experience a hint of its taste, like a memory.

When he came back the next day, the boy brought something else for me. He put it out on the rock but I did not know what it was. Again, I revealed myself to him for just a moment so he'd know I was there. He placed the thing in the air and I brought it closer to my face. It was bigger than the apple, but I knew it was not food. I wasn't sure what to do with it, so I returned it to the boy, hoping he'd show me what it was.

The boy took the thing back and opened it along a hidden fold on one side. "Once upon a time," he said, "there was a mother whose baby was stolen by goblins." I still couldn't understand what his words meant, but I was sure he must be telling me a story. I listened to his distant voice, and loved that he was speaking just to me.

I know it all would have seemed very strange to others. We didn't speak the same language, and we were barely able to see each other with our eyes. I thought he might be called "James" because he said that word as he pointed to himself, though perhaps the word meant "human" in his language. I was not sure, but it didn't matter. What mattered was the swelling in my chest when I saw his little shadow appear on the rock. Even if I didn't always show myself to him, or if I stayed on the other side of the river, he knew I was there. Then, one afternoon, I saw the surface of the water shimmer in an unusual way, and to my surprise it was James in a little boat, coming to see me, and that's when I knew for sure.

I finally had a friend.

THE LIBRARY

·

H is ship arrived one morning and crashed into
the rocks. I rescued him from the salt water and
dragged him onto the beach. His body was so smooth
and strange. He wore something around his neck. I
wasn't sure what type of animal he was at first, but then
I remembered seeing something similar many years earlier, before I was exiled here. It turned out I had rescued
a human boy. The sand in his eyelashes trembled as he
opened his eyes. He stared at me for a moment and then
he spoke: "You have wings."

"I know," I said.

"Are you an angel? Am I dead?"

I didn't think I needed to answer these questions, so I
brought him to my house at the top of the mountain. I'd
built it myself when I'd arrived here three hundred years
ago. The boy slept for a long time. I thought he might
die, but he didn't. When he was well enough, I gave him
new clothes and fed him with fruit from the island.

"Were there any other survivors?" asked the boy.

"I saw no one else," I said. The boy wept.

"Why do you cry?" I asked.

"My father was on the ship. And now . . . I'm alone."

"You are not alone," I said, stating what seemed like a very obvious thing. "I am here."

The boy stared at me, and I could not tell what he was thinking. I had been alone for so long I had nearly forgotten what it was like to have a conversation, so I remained silent for a long time. Then I remembered something he might find of interest.

"I found one other thing from the wreck," I told him. "A locked chest."

The boy sat up. "Where is it now?"

I brought him the chest, and he opened it with the key he wore around his neck.

As he lifted the lid, we saw the trunk was full of seawater stained black with ink and glue. One by one the boy pulled out soaking, ruined books. They dissolved in his hands and he collapsed on the floor in tears.

"Tell me what they were," I asked.

"My father's books," he said. "He was teaching me from them. I loved reading these books and discussing them with him. Now he is gone, and so are all the things he knew. Everything is lost."

The little human boy looked so sad. I wanted to help him. I wanted to be his friend. I had an idea and put out my hand. "Come."

The boy wiped his eyes, took my hand, and stood up.

We walked through my house, hand in hand, until we came to a set of doors at the end of a long hallway. I opened the doors and led him through.

The boy looked around the room. There were thousands of books on shelves that lined the walls from floor to ceiling.

"My library," I said. "You can read whatever you want. Think of it as home."

The boy pulled one of the books off the shelf and opened it.

"This book is handwritten."

"They all are," I said.

"Who wrote them?"

"I did."

"All of them?"

"Yes," I said.

"How long did that take you?"

I didn't think the boy would understand the answer, so I said nothing. He looked again at the book in his hands and began to read out loud. "'The heartbroken giant collapsed and died at the edge of the sea. The world trembled when he fell, and for a hundred years the wind blew salt, and sand, and soil, and seeds across his giant body until it became a mountain. The seeds took root and *a forest grew . . .'"* The boy stopped, then asked, "What *is* this?"

"The story of this island," I answered.

"And what are all the other books?"

"The story of everything else."

Every day, the boy read my books, which pleased me at first. Then he started asking questions. A lot of questions. It became very annoying. He got especially mad at me when I told him his answers could be found in other books elsewhere in the library.

"But what do *you* think the answer is?" he pressed.

"The books *are* what I think," I said. "All my thoughts can be found in these books. Everything that happens can be found here."

"That's not true."

"It is."

"*I* happened," he said, "and I'm not in these books."

"Yes, you are."

"But . . . you wrote these books before I arrived."

I shrugged. "What I mean is that these books contain everything that ever happened, and everything that ever *will* happen. So you're definitely in there."

"You knew I was going to wash up on your shore?"

"At some point, yes. But . . ."

"But what?"

"I don't *remember* what I write."

The boy looked around at the endless rows of books. "Which one am I in?"

I shook my head. I didn't know.

"They're not in *order*?"

I shook my head again.

The boy seemed disgusted by this. "I've never heard of a disorganized library. My father would hate it here. He organized everything very carefully."

"Life isn't organized. Why should my library be any different?"

The boy stood up quickly and grew angry. "What's the point of knowing everything if you forget it and can't even figure out where the answers are? Why don't you just burn down the whole thing? What would it matter?"

He ran out of the room, and I let him go without following. I didn't see him again for a few days, but then one night I passed the open door of the library. Inside, books were strewn around the floor. At first, I thought the boy, wanting some kind of revenge on me, had simply thrown them around the room, but when I looked closer, I realized what he was doing. He was organizing them. It was an impossible task of course, but the gesture touched me somehow.

There was a small shadow by the window, and I saw

the boy sleeping with his head gently resting on the sill. The whisper of a memory came to me, a conversation he and I were going to have the next day. It was a conversation about the ocean, and what he wanted to do, but whether he wanted to stay or to go, I could not remember.

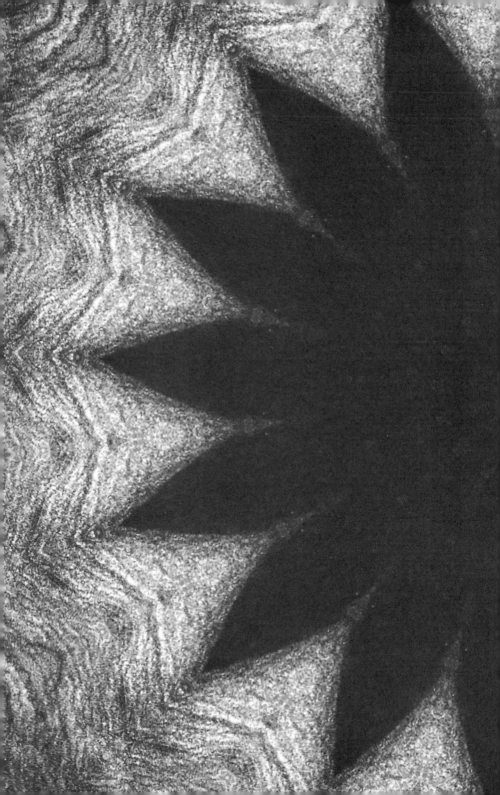

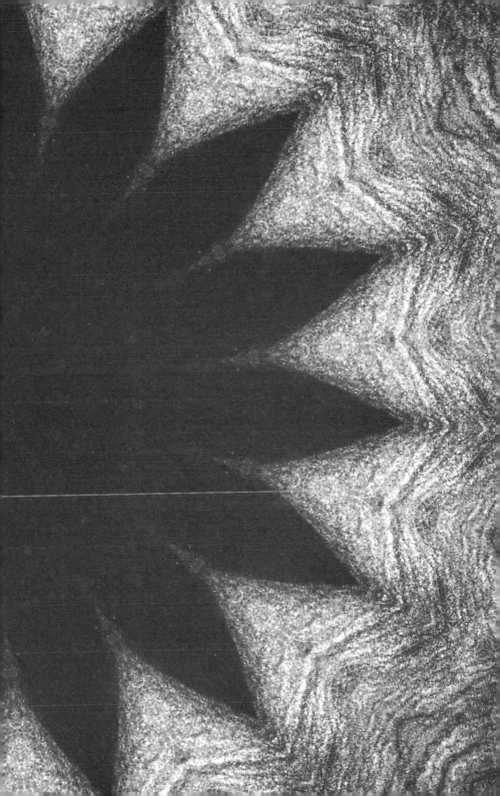

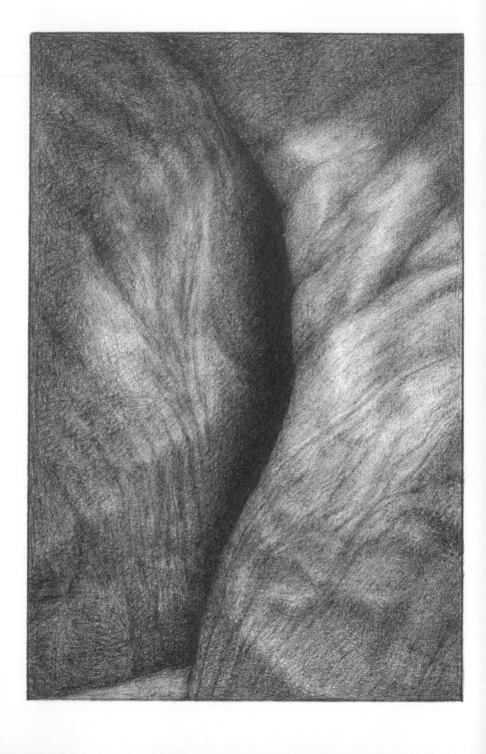

THE GENIE OF THE CAVE

•

I had to climb down a steep cliff to get there. Rocks and sand constantly gave way beneath my feet, and the sun was always strong and hot, but I loved this spot because no one ever came here. I never went in the ocean because I knew the water was full of sharks and things that bite and sting, but I loved looking at the endless waves rolling to the shore and the way the blues were always changing. I'd sneak off from everyone and come here with my books whenever I could. I usually sat with my back against the large rocks that blocked the narrow entrance to a cave cut into the cliff face. There was something forbidding and strange about the black gash, but the shade from the rocks was nice on sunny days.

Not that anyone ever asked me, but all the company I ever needed was a book and the breeze at the edge of the ocean. I was happiest when I was alone. But then, one day, a voice came from nowhere and said, "Hello!"

I jumped and looked around, trying to find the speaker. "Who's there?" I said to the air.

"Behind you," came the voice.

But behind me was only the dark entrance into the

cave. I stood up and turned to the gash in the rocks.

"Is there someone *in* there?" I asked.

"Yes."

"Who are you?"

"I am the Genie of the Cave," said the voice. "I will grant you three wishes."

Now, I am a very rational person. I love science. I subscribe to *Mechanical Monthly*. I keep up-to-date on all the latest inventions and scientific discoveries. I could recite most of the periodic table from memory and I could draw a diagram showing how the telephone works. So when I heard the voice in the cave, I'd like to say I knew right away it couldn't be a real genie. But for a strange moment, I believed it was real, and to be honest, the thought scared me half to death. Because if genies were real, then *anything* could be real. Dragons, giants, creatures from Mars, fairies, witches, and angels could all be released from their books and folktales into the real world like the demons from Pandora's box.

"Hello? I'm talking to you," came the voice again. "Don't ignore the Genie!"

I stood, shaken, and stepped up onto a large rock. I pulled myself toward the opening of the cave and I let my eyes adjust to the darkness. Slowly, I was able to see inside the cavern. The space looked wide and wet and empty. But there, on a rock not too far from me, sat a barefoot boy about my age. His sleeves were rolled up and his shoes were placed neatly on the ground.

"How did you get in there?" I asked.

"I've been in here for a thousand years," he said. "How did you get out there?"

"I climbed down the cliff."

"You'll have to show me sometime. Can you squeeze inside?"

I heaved myself up, and with a little bit of maneuvering, I managed to get through the opening. I found myself inside the cave for the first time, face-to-face with the boy.

"Welcome to my cave," he said. "What is your first wish?"

"You're not a genie."

"How do you know?"

"Because genies are not real. And you don't look like one."

"What do genies look like?" he asked.

I pictured a genie from a storybook I had as a little kid, wearing a turban with jewels, floating up out of a lamp. "Well, they don't look like *you*," I said.

"Is what something looks like all that matters?"

"Well, no, of course not," I said. "That's not what I'm saying."

"You're saying you don't believe in genies."

"Yes."

"What about elephants?"

"What about them?"

"Do you believe in elephants?"

"Of course I believe in elephants."

"Why?"

"Because they're real!"

"Have you ever seen one?"

"Yes."

"You have?"

"*Pictures* of them."

"In books," he said. "Like genies?"

"You're very annoying," I said.

The boy shrugged. "Want a tour of my cave?"

He slid down from the rock he was sitting on and, to my surprise, took my hand. I followed him deep inside the cave.

"Don't let go of me," he said.

"Why?"

"The light doesn't reach back here. I know my way around, so trust me."

We ducked down and went through a long tunnel before we were able to stand up again. The darkness was complete. All I could feel was the boy's hand and the ground beneath my feet.

I could hear our breathing and water dripping from somewhere, and I could smell the salt from the sea. The air was cool against my skin, and we walked for a while until we stopped moving. I was about to ask why we'd stopped, but at that moment he squeezed my hand tightly, and somehow, I understood he was communicating to me without words. He was saying: *You don't need to speak now.*

We stood side by side, holding hands. I thought about an hourglass, where the sand is pouring down from above until the top half is empty. My head felt like the top half of the hourglass, and I could feel everything pouring out—my thoughts, my memories, my past, all the books I'd read, all the diagrams of telephones I'd memorized, my family, my dreams, my fears. I was dissolving and becoming something new. I existed only in the place where the palm of my hand touched his. This connection was the only thing left: the heat from his hand, and the way his fingers would loosen slightly, then get tighter but never let go. I believed that if he pulled away his hand, I would float into outer space and vanish among the stars. But his hand didn't go away. It held tight.

Time no longer existed and there were no boundaries between things. I heard a voice and didn't know if the boy had spoken, or if I'd imagined it, or if I'd spoken the words myself.

"Make your first wish," the voice said.

But it was already coming true.

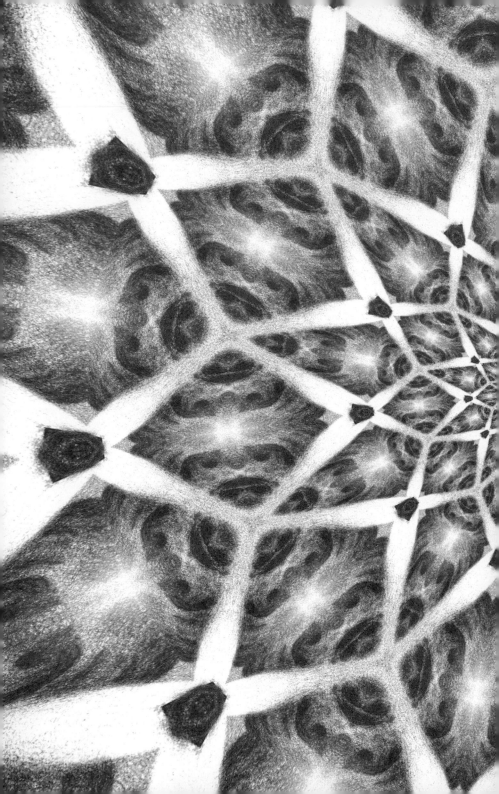

THE ICE

•

I lived in the nice house James built for me in Kensington. I know he loved me because he also made me tables and chairs and sewed me clothes and told me all his secrets. My house had many rooms, and sometimes there were spiders. I did not like the spiders. They were very large and spun webs in my house, but James cleaned them out. My house was on the floor of his attic, which is one of the rooms in *his* house. His house was so big I could not even imagine it. I fit comfortably in the palm of James. From my house I was able to see out a window in his attic. I could see blue, which James said was the sky.

At night when the sky went away, James visited me with candles and told me stories from books he carried. I liked the stories James told to me. James said I was a secret. That meant no one, not even Father, knew I lived in the attic. Only James.

James told me many things about Father. James belonged to Father the way I belonged to James. Father had heavy shoes and expensive things that James was not allowed to touch. But James told me the expensive things were shiny, so he touched them anyway and made Father mad. When Father was by the fire, James wanted to sit near him, to hear stories, to hold his big hand. But Father said, "No." Father always said, "No." I would never say "No" to James, even if I could talk out loud.

One day James began to prepare me for a big trip.

"You're going to have an adventure," he whispered to me. "You're going on a ship. You'll see the stars, and you will sleep under the moon as you cross the world."

I tried to imagine what that would be like but I could not. I wanted James to come with me, but James said he was going elsewhere. He could not go where I was going. I had to go alone.

James made me a special jacket, and inside the jacket he placed a folded piece of paper with tiny words. He read the note to me and then gave me directions.

"Deliver this note to Father when you are out to sea," he said. "Do you promise to do that?"

I promised in my heart.

"I will miss you, but I know you are brave," James said.

I was happy to learn I was brave.

I was in the hand of James when he said goodbye to his Father. The hand of James slipped me into the pocket of Father's coat.

His Father did not know I was there.

Then he found me and pulled me from his pocket.

For a brief moment I could see the ship and the sails.
I could feel the wind on my face and see a sky that looked
like the sky in the attic window, but much, much bigger.

I could hear voices.

"What's that?" said one of them.

"I don't know," said the Father. His dark eyes looked
down at me as I lay in his large rough hand. "My son
must have made it. He's always making little things and
leaving them around the house. I guess he snuck it into
my pocket before I left. He's a strange boy."

I did not know James was a strange boy.

I tried to tell the Father about the note in my pocket
that James wanted me to deliver, but the Father did not
look inside my jacket. He returned me to his pocket.

The ship was moving, and then there were very loud
sounds like explosions and the ship stopped moving.

I could hear men talking about The Ice.

Everyone was talking about The Ice.

There was so much Ice it was all anyone could talk
about.

The Ice meant the ship could not move anymore.

The Ice meant everyone talked about death. They
said they did not want to die.

I didn't know what death was. I wondered if I could do it. I wondered if *James* could die.

I felt the Father running and heard dogs barking.

There was screaming.

I did not know what was happening, but there was more talking and loud breathing.

Everything stopped, including the breathing. There was only the sound of wind.

It was very cold.

Time passed, but I had no way of knowing how much. I was never very aware of time.

"It's a miracle," said a new voice. "We found them."

There was the blue sky again. After so much darkness, it felt more beautiful than it ever had before. But I could feel something else too . . . a kind of joy that was almost the same as the joy of seeing James.

New hands. More people. I was wrapped in the softest white fabric, and for the first time in a long time I was not cold.

Another ship. A long journey.

I was unwrapped and placed on a tray on a clean silver table. Everything was very bright. There were three people standing above me. They wore white gloves and touched me very gently as if I might break at any moment. One of them talked to me and said they'd take good care of me. I said thank you and asked where I was, but they didn't answer.

One of them said, "How old do you think it is?"

"Well, the shipwreck was in 1845. That's a hundred and seventy-five years ago."

"Wow."

"It's in perfect condition."

"The ice preserved it, along with the bodies of the men."

They took off my jacket.

"What's that?" one of them said as the note to the Father fell onto the table.

"Is that a tiny piece of paper?"

"It's folded."

"Be careful with it."

I hoped they would finally give the note to the Father, but they did not. They unfolded it and held it up beneath a magnifying glass.

"Well," said the one with the magnifying glass, "it might have said something once, but the words have long since disappeared."

Now I am in a glass case in a museum. I am very comfortable because there is a hidden support behind my back. The air in here is very clean and the temperature is always the same. The piece of paper with the note from James was folded up and returned to the inside of my jacket. I am the only one who knows what it said. There is now a sign beside me that tells the story of the ship I was on, and the explorers who died in the snow. All day long, people look through the glass at me. They stop and read the story on the glass and point.

I cannot hear what they say, but I look at their faces, and wait each day for James.

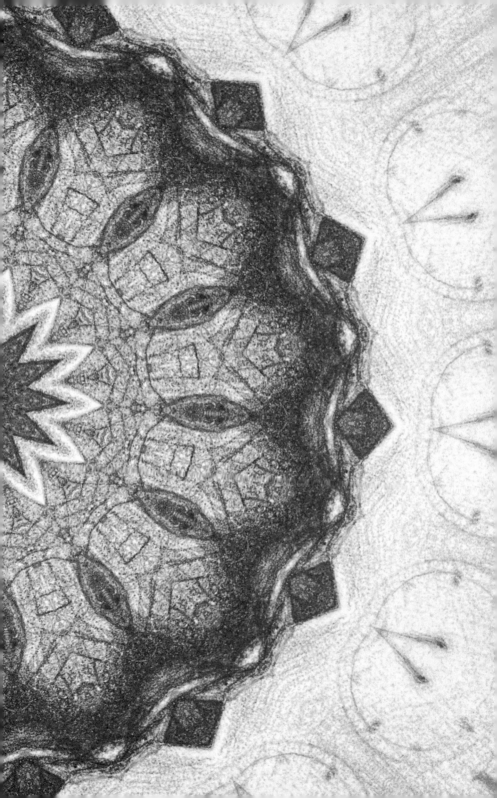

THE ABANDONED HOUSE

·

W e moved from room to room, unlatching the shutters over the windows. Cold bright morning light cut through the dust in the air like knives. Vines had broken through the glass and spread across the walls, and it looked in places as if the wallpaper had come to life. There was a carpet of dried leaves on the floor, which crunched beneath our feet as we walked. Small animals heard our footsteps and scurried under the furniture. Spiders had spun vast shimmering webs that flourished with the absence of human hands. It felt as if the border between indoors and outdoors had dissolved, and I'd never been happier in my life

James cleared out a fireplace and lit the fire, which was especially satisfying since his parents never let him touch matches at home. Soon the room had warmed up and we sat cross-legged on the leafy ground.

"No one knows this place is here," James said.

"It's ours now," I answered, picking up a pine cone and rolling its spiky edges against my palm.

"Let's live here forever," James said.

"Okay," I answered, as if it was true.

"But don't tell anyone."

"Our secret."

He put out his hand and I gave him the pine cone. He tossed it into the fire.

I looked at a broken clock leaning against one of the walls. The hands were lost and the glass was broken. The metal weights had fallen, and the rusted chains that once held them in place were nearly indistinguishable from the wild tendrils that grew upward out of the floor.

James saw me staring at the ruins of the clock.

"I think it's broken," I said with a smile.

"Maybe not."

"What?"

"I mean, clocks tell time, right?" James didn't take his eyes from the clock. "So don't you think this one is still telling time?"

"That clock is definitely not telling time." I laughed.

"Well, it used to tell time in seconds and minutes and hours, and it doesn't do that anymore. Now it tells time in decades, and centuries."

"I don't understand what you're talking about," I said.

"Most people think time is a machine that needs to be oiled and wound with a key. They think it's something you control and maintain. But maybe it's more *wild* than that. Maybe it's bigger and stranger. Maybe time is uncontrollable, and endless, and . . . dangerous. Like a forest eating a house."

I looked around the crumbling room and tried to really understand what James was talking about. But time, and James, were mysteries to me, and I wondered if I'd ever figure either of them out.

At that moment James and I both heard something. There was an odd tapping on the other side of the room. We discovered it was coming from a tall cabinet that stood near the windows. The sound was like fingers drumming against the wood from the inside. On the doors of the cabinet, someone had long ago carved a great sailing ship rolling on an endless ocean. The tapping seemed to get louder.

"Don't," I said as James put his hands on the wooden knobs.

He opened the doors. To our surprise, a hundred blue butterflies burst all at once from the cabinet, their damp broken chrysalises still dangling upside down from the undersides of the uneven shelves. The warmth of the fire and the opened shutters must have woken them from their slumber, and they fluttered into the air with joy.

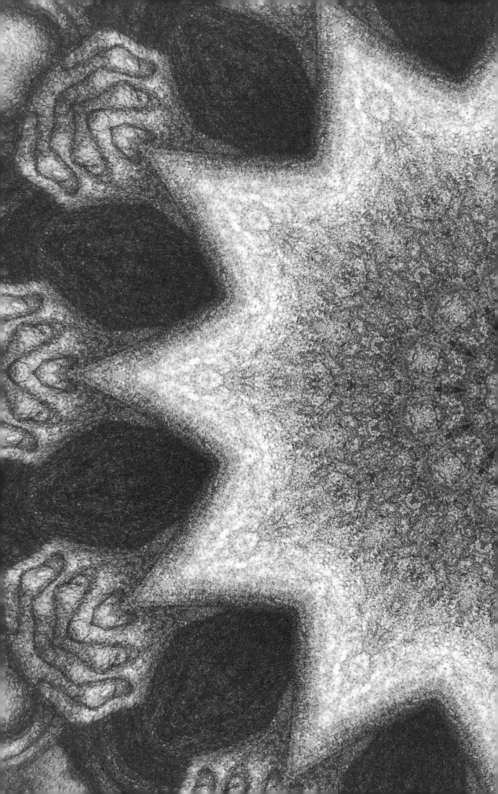

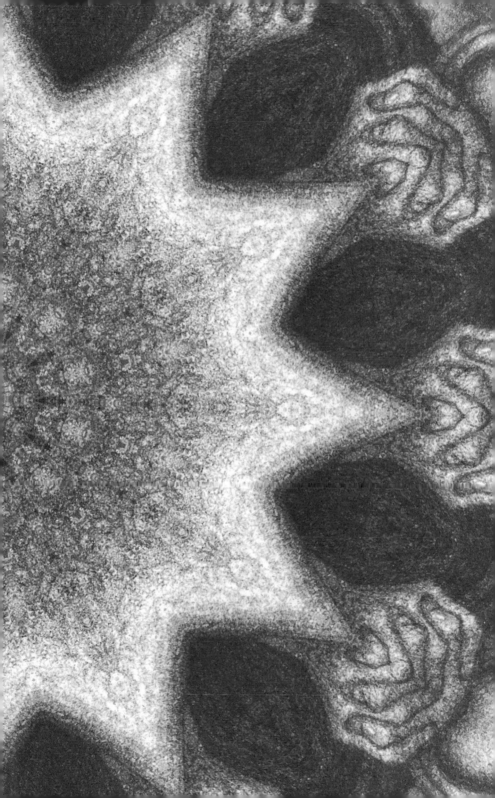

THE SPIRIT MACHINE

•

T he machine sat on your dining room table, intricate and gleaming. Each piece had been made by hand with great care—the brass, the wood, the silver, the spun copper wires, the ornate glass knobs. There was a kind of hum that seemed to emanate from the machine, and the room felt alive and full of potential, though all of that energy may have been coming from you.

You'd been working on the Spirit Machine for months, hammering and tinkering in your workshop, adding new parts, adjusting the wires, and touching up the paint. You believed that one day this machine would allow you to talk to the dead. You thought it would galvanize the electricity in the air like a kind of battery, causing a reaction that would break down the barrier between the living and the dead.

You did it all for me.

It seemed as if sparks were always flying out the windows of your workshop, and sometimes the whole shack filled with smoke. The children in the area thought a witch was living in the woods, mixing potions and making spells day and night. Even though you kept the door and windows locked, the constant vibrations of the tools had loosened some of the nails holding the slats of wood onto the walls, and those same children soon were trying to look through the gaps. No one knew what you were making in that little shack in the back of your property, but you'd burn piles of paper and scraps of wood beneath the stars, and the smoke and the sparks and the fire made the adults in town wonder if you were doing something sinister.

The idea for the Spirit Machine had come to you in a dream. You'd been mourning me a long time, and your grief was threatening to wreck you. The morning of the dream, you woke up with a start. You had scrambled through your bedroom, stumbling to find paper and a pencil. The image stayed firm in your mind and you drew it in a kind of fever. You'd never had an experience like that before, and you were shaken by it. You remembered Jacob wrestling all night with an angel, who finally blessed him as the sun rose in the morning.

I knew you better than anyone else in the world. I knew how deeply you felt things, how frustrated you became when you felt powerless.

Nothing makes living people feel more powerless than Death.

The creation of the Spirit Machine gave you a

newfound feeling of purpose and pride. It helped you focus your energy and your grief. You used all your skills to build it, and learned new ones as well. You drew detailed plans based on the image from your dream. You cut down trees from the woods behind your home and carefully carved and joined each piece, using knives and lathes and drills. You blew the glass, hammered the copper, fashioned the ceramic spools, and meticulously painted the entire thing with sable-hair brushes you made yourself. You weren't just building a machine, you were making a work of art, a moving sculpture and a scientific invention all at once. It was the most beautiful thing I'd ever seen.

I don't remember very much about being alive. I don't remember the moment I died, and I don't remember most of the things I did. But I remember you. You thought you needed the machine to bring me back. You thought if you couldn't see me I was not present, if you couldn't hear me I was not speaking to you, if you couldn't feel me we could not touch. You thought the machine would change all that, but I was already with you. I didn't need a device to be there. You yourself were the Spirit Machine. You were the thing that tied me to the world.

What will happen after you die. I do not know.

You invited the curious children who had snuck around

your workshop to see the finished machine. They told their parents about the strange creation, and many of the parents came to see it as well. Soon, visitors from out of town were coming to take a look. Most people didn't understand what it was, and many thought you were crazy, but somehow everyone understood that you had taken your sadness and loss and made something beautiful out of it. You met artists, scientists, and dreamers, and you engaged in long conversations and exchanged fascinating letters with authors and philosophers for years afterward. In a way, I believe it saved your life . . . and if you want to know a secret, that's why I gave you the dream in the first place.

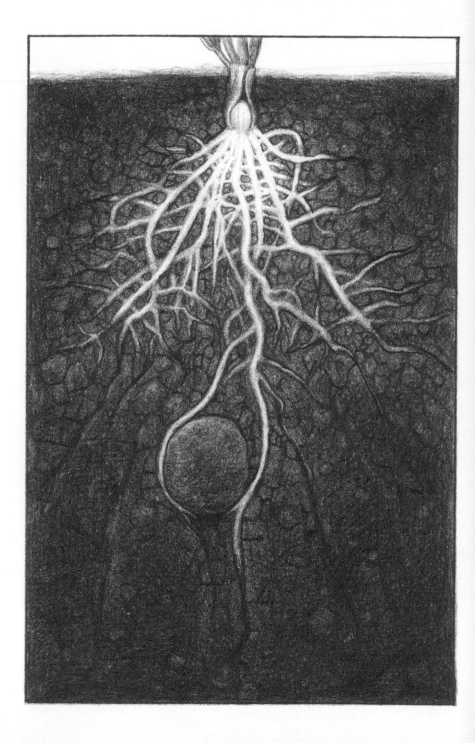

THE QUEST

·

When I was younger, my cousin the archduke invited me to go sledding at his villa. I was frightened because I'd never seen snow before, but he told me to hold his coat tightly as we sped down the hill. Later that evening, sitting by his fire, he told me stories about the lush green forests that once filled my kingdom, but I didn't believe him. Brown grass and dusty rocks had covered the hills of my homeland for as long as I could remember. It was like a graveyard cut into the middle of paradise, a salted garden. I ruled over a dead kingdom from a broken palace at the top of an eroding hill.

It was a spring morning when the knight first appeared on my dusty horizon, his ruby-encrusted armor gleaming in the sun like a burning meteor come down to earth. When he was close enough, I saw lilacs engraved on his chest plate. He told me he'd been on a quest for many years, but he'd begun to dream of this place, and me. So he gave up his quest and traveled across continents and sailed across oceans to get here.

"You're a madman," I said. "There is nothing here but death and loneliness."

"But *you* are here," he said as he took my hand and offered me a gift. It was a young tree, maybe eighteen inches tall, and foreign to this area. I apologized and told him nothing would grow here. But he smiled a mysterious smile and said he'd had a vision. The tree would grow.

Together, the knight and I planted the tree, and then we planted more. We hand-watered the saplings and cared for them like children. As they grew they shed their leaves, and the soil slowly absorbed the nutrients. Eventually, we were able to plant even more trees, which firmly took root, and as the decades passed they reached upward to the sky. Birds and animals arrived with the spreading of the forest. The sounds of my kingdom were transformed from the hollow ache of wind to the mysterious songs of nightingales and the endless rustle of the leaves. The cold smell of lifeless dirt became a symphony of flowers and sweet perfumes. There was the dark tang of mushrooms and wet soil. The light turned emerald green and a thousand species of multicolored butterflies flitted from branch to branch like a shattered rainbow.

The knight and I built a small home in the valley, leaving my palace to fall. We continued to plant more trees every day and he said the forest reminded him of his childhood. His fearful mother had raised him deep in the woods, far from other people, in order to keep him safe. But he'd happened upon three wandering knights as they bathed in a lake near his home, and he'd been filled with a sudden desire to become a knight himself. His mother, who had long feared this moment, fainted when he told her he was leaving to become a knight.

One day when the two of us were walking through our forest, we passed the very first tree we'd put into the ground. It had grown so large that we could not reach our arms around the trunk and touch hands. I was reminded of the day he'd first arrived in his gleaming ruby armor, when this had been a dead valley. He'd given up his quest to come here.

He'd never said he would stay forever, but we had grown a forest together, and I couldn't imagine this place without him. He walked ahead of me, and I tried to ignore the crashing sound of the waves, and the thought of his ship, still anchored just off the shore.

Part Two

AFTERNOON

.

THE TUNNEL

•

J ames had always kept his house a secret, but now he was gone and there was something I had to do. The train ride was long and my bags were heavy. I arrived midafternoon. The station was abandoned, except for an old man in a tattered coat who eventually pointed me in the right direction. I followed long roads through tall trees that rose up in gray masses like giants in the mist. And then I finally saw it . . . James's house.

I'm not sure what I had been expecting, but as the haze lifted, I realized his house looked very much like a castle. It was vast and dark, with turrets rising on one side. I could feel the blood coursing through my body like rivers through a landscape, my heart beating with trepidation as I got closer. A car was parked in front, heavy-looking and expensive. The portico had two giant wood doors beneath it. I took note of their curling, twisting iron hinges and their handles, with loops of metal that seemed wider than my head. Columns with flowering caps bordered the doors, and above them was a long marble panel with a sculpted elephant, its trunk pointing up toward the sky. I walked to the doors and pulled the handles, but they didn't budge. I knocked. It made a hollow sound, like I was knocking on the door of a tomb. I tried to imagine James, years ago, sleeping in some ornate bedroom inside, but nothing came to mind. I thought I heard footsteps behind me, but when I turned, no one was there.

I walked along the edge of the huge building and saw myself reflected in the tall glass windows. The perfectly cut lawn sloped upward, away from the house. I scanned the grounds for the flashing eyes. In the distance I saw a fountain with a small star-shaped pool.

At the far end of the building, I discovered the entrance to a passageway for carriages that seemed to lead directly *under* the house. There was an ornate metal gate guarding the entrance with an imposing black lock. I could have easily squeezed between the bars but the tunnel scared me. For years I'd had nightmares about being lost in long, dark corridors, as if I was stuck inside the Minotaur's labyrinth.

I circled the entire house, trying to find another way inside, but every door and every window was locked. I stumbled across the grass and ended up back at the entrance to the tunnel.

I didn't know what to do, but then I heard the rumble of a storm in the distance as the sun vanished completely behind dark clouds. I looked through the metal bars. Behind me was thunder and wild animals, and in front of me, darkness. I couldn't stop thinking about my nightmares, but I knew if I allowed myself to plunge in, I might find a way into the house.

I held my breath, squeezed through the bars, and entered the tunnel.

In moments, I could see nothing at all. I kept my right hand on the wall and took small steps, in case the floor suddenly gave way beneath me. There was a strange musty smell in the passageway, and I could detect mud and rotting wood and something metallic in the air. My fingers felt every bump and crevice in the stones of the wall. The world was reduced to what I could feel with my fingertips and under the soles of my shoes. I was aware of dirt and slime and water. I heard drips and creaks and a pounding sound that never grew fainter no matter how far into the passageway I walked. Eventually, I realized the sound was my own heartbeat.

Then I felt something brush against my leg and I knew I was not alone. I ran as fast as I could, trying desperately to keep my hand on the wall.

I imagined rabid dogs coming after me, and swarms of bats flying through the darkness. It felt like ghosts were everywhere now and rats were closing in around my feet. Time seemed to break. There was no past and no future. Only this tunnel existed, and this blackness, in this one long, impossible moment.

A thousand years passed with every breath I took. The sun had died and the stars had extinguished themselves. The universe had collapsed, and I was still inside the tunnel, still touching the stones, still holding my suitcase.

Until . . .

Something round and gritty was sticking out of the wall. I grabbed on to it like I was about to drown. A rusted knob.

My fingers became a vise and I turned the knob as hard as I could. I threw my full weight against the wall, and I heard a crack. Pain shot through my arm. I could hear hinges creaking, and something in the wall gave way. A door into the house came open, but no lights came on. The temperature changed, and new smells surrounded me. I was inside, but the darkness continued, so on I went. Inching, I hoped, toward forgiveness.

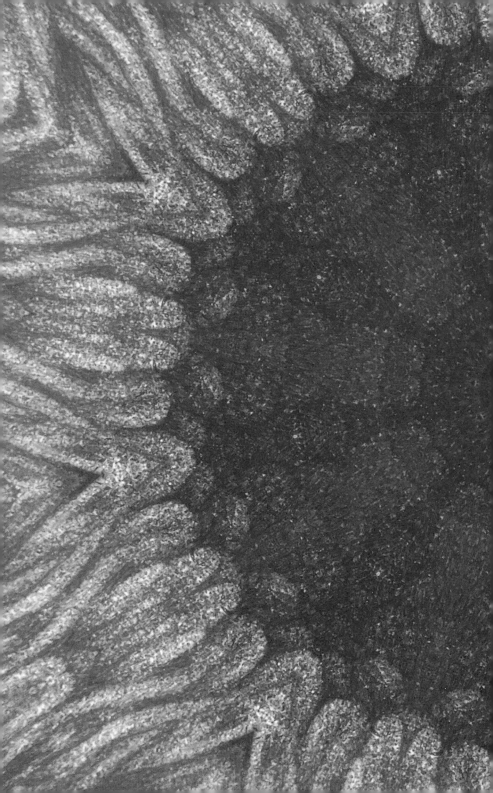

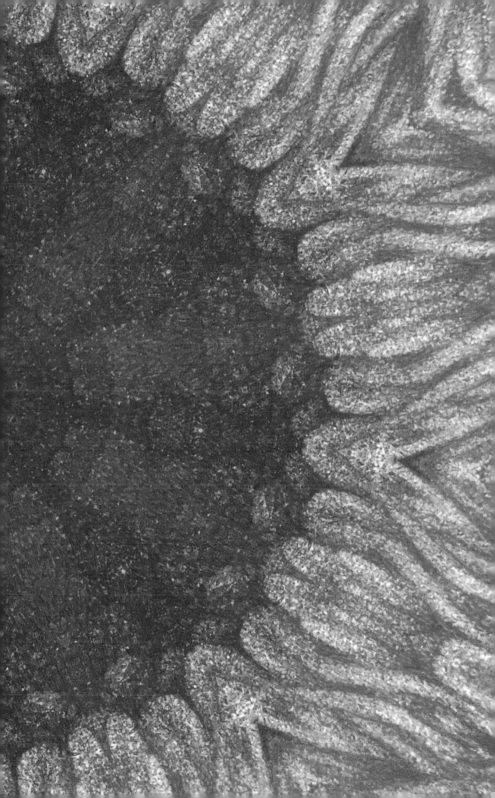

THE LAST TIME
IT HAPPENED

•

T he first time it happened, we were in the cathedral,
which had been closed for repair work. James and I
snuck into the building one afternoon, entering through
a broken basement window. I can't remember why we
decided to do this, considering neither of us would have
gone into the building when it was open. But doing something secret with a friend is always fun.

We made our way through the dark basement until
we found a narrow staircase and climbed upstairs. A
small wood door opened into a corner of the nave, and we
walked straight into the giant space. The echo of our shoe
heels bounced around the walls, and dim red light filtered
in from high, unseen windows. There seemed to be no
ceiling above us. Instead, great arching canopies of stone
soared overhead like the branches of a petrified forest.

"James," I whispered. "Look! The branches . . .
they're moving."

"What are you talking about?" he said. "What
branches? We're *inside*."

I couldn't describe to him what I saw next. The vaults of marble above me began to ripple and breathe, as if a wind was blowing through the forest, and then the wind turned into a hurricane inside my mind and the next thing I knew I was on the floor, capsized. The stone was cold beneath my skin, and my eyes were closed. The darkness was a relief. James rushed to my side and lifted my head to his knee.

"Are you alright?" he asked.

"I don't know," I answered.

The second time it happened, I was in school looking at a painting of an angel in a book. The rainbow-colored wings began to shimmer and I thought I saw them move. I'm not sure if it was a reflection on the page, but it was as if there was no more picture, and no more book—just me and the angel, breathing and alive. A hurricane swept through my mind again, and when I opened my eyes the class was looking down at me in shock.

The third time it happened, I was at home reading about the Minotaur's labyrinth in *Greek Mythology*. The description of the long corridors, the twists and turns, the darkness, the inability to know when the monster would leap out to get me, all of it was so vivid in my mind that I felt as if I was actually inside the labyrinth itself, running and running. The experience was so vivid. Theseus had unraveled a spool of Ariadne's thread as he moved through the maze so he could find his way out, but I had no thread. I was alone, and afraid, and everything went black.

The last time it happened, I was looking at a bird through a window. The black feathers were very beautiful and the shiny black eyes stared back at me. Then there was a rush and I was no longer looking at the bird. I was looking at *myself* through the window from the outside, and somehow I knew that I was now the bird. My head twitched to the side. I felt a stretch and then I was leaping off the windowsill and soaring up into the sky. I could see the clouds above. The rushing air against my feathers made my entire body shiver. Down below were red treetops and roofs, snaking roads and twisting rivers with tiny, wind-tossed boats. There was a sound in my ears that must have been made by the wind but somehow it seemed more like music. I was always aware of the sun, even when I could not see it. I knew where I was flying to. I was not thinking. I just *knew* things. I knew to turn left. I knew to rise up. I knew to dive down. There was no fear, but there was also no curiosity. And that's when I realized there was also no beauty and no ugliness. There was only the world.

And then it was over and I was sitting at my window, looking out into the blue sky.

I wonder if any of it was real. Could I have truly seen a cathedral tremble or a painting of an angel breathe? Could I have been lost inside a labyrinth? Was I really once a bird?

Whenever the questions keep me up at night, I hear James whisper in my ear. He says, "Yes," and "Yes," and "Yes," and "Yes."

THE MUSEUM

·

We followed our teacher through the museum toward a bright room where we were instructed to sit on the floor before a giant painting of the Garden of Eden. It was almost as tall as the room itself. Peacocks, lions, sheep, and elephants wandered around enchanted green hills while a green serpent wound its way through the Tree of Knowledge, which hung with red fruit in the center of the garden. An apple, bitten and discarded, lay beneath the tree, half-hidden in the grass. Off to the right, unnoticed by any of the animals, Adam and Eve were being expelled in shame by an angel with rainbow-colored wings. A burning sword hovered in the air above him.

I was intrigued by the painting of the garden, but I was having trouble concentrating. I was thinking about the dream I'd had the night before. There had been a boy with big dark eyes who I'd never seen before.

My teacher bored me and I wanted to explore the rest of the museum on my own. Everyone was looking at the painting, so it was easy to sneak away. I soon found myself in a long dark corridor where the sounds of the museum completely fell away. The air was still and calm. Up ahead I spotted an unmarked entrance to a dark, little room. Something compelled me to step inside.

The room was empty except for a single glass case in the middle of the floor. Inside the case, lying on its back with its arms bound to its sides, its blank eyes staring upward, was an ancient mummy. A faint glow seemed to emanate from it, like the edge of an eclipse. I kneeled down. The stone floor was cold against my knees. I stared hard at the linen-wrapped body, and I imagined its chest rising and falling, rising and falling, as if it were breathing.

I knew that was impossible, but I thought I heard a sound from inside the glass. I pressed my ear against the case and listened. Yes, I was sure I heard something, a distant breath, so faint it almost wasn't there at all.

And then the mummy spoke.

"Hello," it said, and I was so startled I almost fell over as I jumped back. I caught myself and saw something on the other side of the case. A boy was staring back at me through the glass. It was his voice I'd heard.

His dark eyes shined, and there was something strangely familiar about him.

"I come here a lot," he said. "I've never seen you before."

"It's my first time."

"What were you doing?"

"Listening."

"To what?"

I pointed into the glass case.

"The mummy?" he asked.

I nodded.

"What did you hear?"

"Breathing."

"That might have been me," he said. "I have asthma."

Suddenly I realized why he seemed familiar to me.

"I think you were in my dream last night," I said to him.

He smiled.

"Why are you smiling?" I asked.

"Because I think it's magical if you appear in someone else's dreams. Don't you?"

"I don't know."

"Hasn't anyone ever dreamed about *you*?"

"I don't think so."

"I'll try to dream about you tonight," the boy said before he turned once again to the case. "Do you think mummies can dream?"

"Don't you have to be *alive* to dream?"

The boy thought for a moment. "We dream about

the dead, and it's like they come back to life. So I don't see why the dead can't dream about us."

"That doesn't make any sense."

The boy shrugged. "Maybe she's dreaming about us right now."

There was something so compelling about the way the boy spoke that for a moment I almost believed that he and I, as well as this entire museum and the universe itself, had been conjured into being by this ancient queen. Then an adult voice echoed from the far end of the corridor and I snapped back to the real world.

"James!" called the voice. "Where are you?"

"That's me," he said. "I have to go. Can you meet me here tomorrow?"

"No," I said, disappointed. "I'm on a class trip. I don't think we're coming back."

"James!" came the voice once more.

"I want to see you again," I told him.

"You will," he assured me as he stood to leave.

"When?" I asked.

"Tonight," he answered as he ran off.

That night, alone in my bed, I could still see the mummy's eyelids, thin as tissue, and the color of dust. Three thousand years ago she had seen the pyramids and the Nile. She had felt the Egyptian sun on her skin, and as I fell asleep I tried to imagine myself three thousand years in the future. What would I be dreaming of?

I opened my eyes and the boy was there, waiting for me in the shadow of a colossal Sphinx, an apple in his hand.

THE STORY OF
MR. GARDNER

•

When James and I were growing up in New Jersey, there was a strange man who lived across the street from me named Mr. Gardner. The light in his attic stayed on all the time, but no one knew anything about him. He was a mystery. Then, one afternoon, we came back to my house and saw a police car and an ambulance in his driveway. Mr. Gardner had died, and when his obituary was published in the local paper a few days later, the neighborhood discovered what he'd been doing in his attic all those years. Mr. Gardner, we learned, had filled his house with reference books. He'd begun the collection with travel books years ago after his wife became ill. Neither of them had ever left the East Coast, but it gave her comfort to dream of seeing the world. Then Mr. Gardner found an old atlas and gave it to his wife as a birthday present, and after that, the collection grew rapidly. His wife had always loved reading, so they began collecting dictionaries and thesauri. Soon there were piles of encyclopedias in ancient languages as well, and maps of the stars, and roomfuls of biographies. At some point they added almanacs and phone books and directories and manuals to machines that no one had used in a hundred years.

After his wife died, Mr. Gardner apparently grew unsatisfied with the collection. It was too big, too overwhelming. He told his sister he was going to write his own reference book, a single volume that would contain all the information in the universe, which he would dedicate to the memory of his wife. He went up to his attic, sat down at his desk, and typed the word *apple* on a piece of paper, probably thinking that was as good a place to start as any. But as he tried to define the word, he found himself also having to define so many other things, like the color red (which itself was nearly impossible to define), and the idea of seeds, and the concept of shiny, and the taste of something delicious. He found that he had to write about supermarkets, and the concept of sin, because he remembered Eve ate the apple in the Garden of Eden. He wrote about Snow White, who ate a poisoned apple, and he wrote about the smell of the apple pies his grandmother baked when he was young. When they found him dead in his attic room, he'd been working on his book for over twenty years. He was surrounded by seventy-five thousand pieces of paper, still trying to finish his definition of an apple.

There was some talk that a local museum would try to save the book, but a group of boys broke into the house one afternoon and set the place on fire. The pages from Mr. Gardner's book burned fast and bright. Some of them, as if they were trying to escape, floated up past the burning walls of the house. They drifted on the heated air and landed in my yard like snow. James and I collected as many of the pages as we could and brought them inside. They were charred and smelled of smoke, but we boxed them up and put them safely away. After that, when we were alone after school, we'd open the box and read from Mr. Gardner's definition of an apple. There were stories and ideas that clearly linked to the apple, like Johnny Appleseed, or a page with the history of a town in Scotland that I realized had something to do with the word *Macintosh*, which is a type of apple. But other pieces of paper had writing I could in no way connect with apples. James and I read these scraps to each other, as if they were from a magician's book of spells. *"'Regarding the migration of butterflies,'"* James read out loud, *"'the trip is so long, and their life-spans are so short, that it takes them five generations to get there. Imagine leaving for vacation but it's your great-great-great-grandchild who arrives.'"*

"Is that true?" I asked.

"Yes," said James. He knew a lot about butterflies.

We had only a tiny fraction of everything he wrote in our possession, but the fragments included references to Greek myths, the origins of the universe, children's fantasy novels, the quests of King Arthur's knights, the creation of the periodic table, a man who found the entrance to a buried city behind a wall in his house, spaceships, ancient Egypt, mysterious castles, the invention of the kaleidoscope, and the knitted blankets of his childhood bed.

"It's sad that Mr. Gardner died without finishing," I said.

"I suppose," said James. "But I think he may have discovered something interesting."

I waited for James to continue. He gently placed his hand on top of the pile of papers, as if he was touching a living thing, and said, "The entire universe can be found inside an apple."

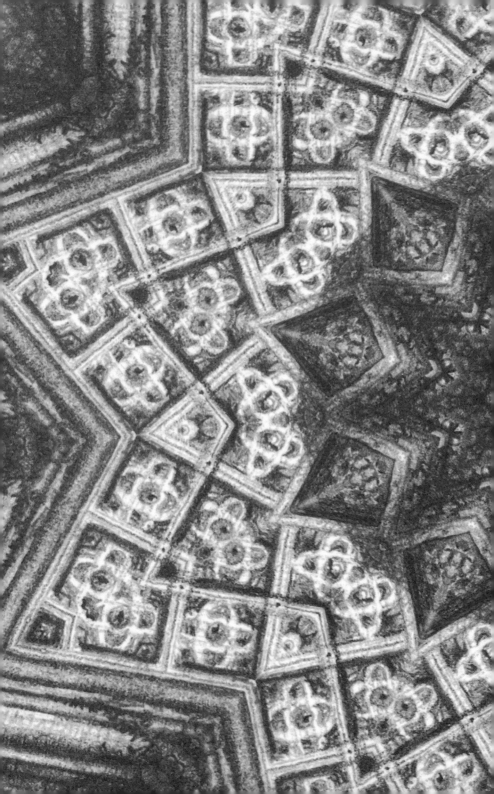

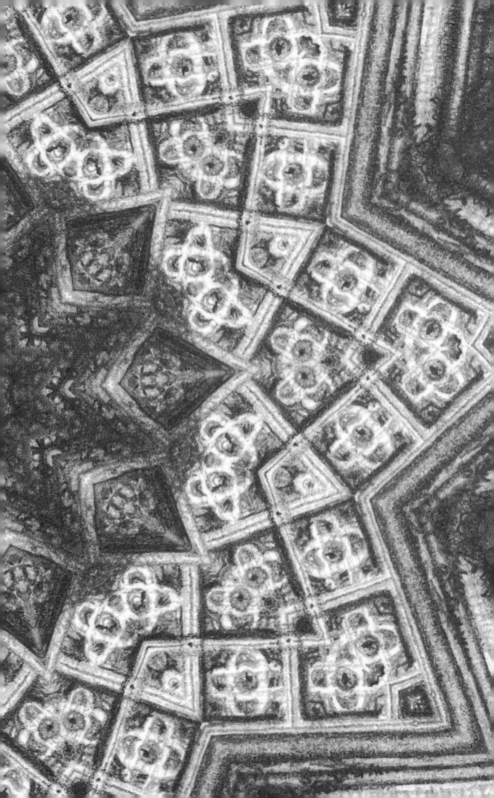

THE LIGHTNING-STRUCK
TREE

•

Opening my eyes, I saw a man standing over me with an axe. I screamed and leapt to my feet. The man screamed too and stumbled backward. Bright sunlight streamed through the door as he dropped his axe, and I quickly realized he wasn't a man. He was just a boy, about my age, and he looked frightened. His sleeves were rolled up to the top of his arms and he was sweating. I could smell newly cut grass and wet earth, and he was staring at me.

"Who are you?" I asked him.

He picked up his axe. His arm was shiny and damp, and it strained under the weight. "You scared me," he said as he smiled and took a step closer to me. "I find wild animals here in the shed sometimes. Raccoons, squirrels. Lots of mice. Once I found a baby deer when I forgot to shut the door. But I've never found a human before. You *are* human, aren't you?"

"What else would I be?"

"Not sure," he said. "You might be a changeling, by the looks of you, left by goblins in the night. This forest is full of strange things. So you never know."

"I was out walking and I got tired," I explained. "The door was open, so I came in and took a nap." Suddenly a memory came to me and I gasped.

"What is it?" he asked me.

"Nothing. It's just—"

"What?"

"I just remembered the dream I was having when you woke me."

"What was it?"

I rubbed my eyes. I could see it as clear as day in my mind. "There was a tree, and it got hit by lightning."

The boy took a step back in alarm. "That wasn't a dream," he said, sounding shocked.

"Yes, it was."

"No, I mean, in the garden last night. A tree was hit by lightning during the storm. It's still burning. That's why I came to get the axe from the shed." The boy stared at me as if I really was a changeling, or a magician. "I told you this forest was full of strange things." He took my hand. "Follow me."

We ran through the forest until we came to a long stone wall. The boy then reached into his pocket and produced an iron key. "Stole it from a witch," he said. "This is her garden. No one's been inside for a hundred years. Except me."

He brushed aside some thick vines, revealing a hidden door. He slid the key into the rusted lock. The click was sharp and satisfying as he turned the key and the door opened.

There, standing alone at the far end of the garden, was a huge tree, split up the middle. It was glowing red and orange *from the inside.*

"See? It's still on fire," the boy said.

It was exactly like my dream.

"Are you going to chop it down?" I asked as we walked toward the tree.

"No, it'll survive. All trees are dead on the inside. It's only the outside that's alive. The axe is for cutting up the branches that fell."

We watched as the flames shifted and flickered upward through the opening in the tree, and we moved closer until I could feel the heat of the flames against my skin.

And then I watched as the boy spotted something in the grass. He bent over and picked up a thin blue feather, pocketed it, and looked back toward the garden door. He made a clicking sound with his tongue. After a moment, two flashing eyes appeared in the doorway. Standing there, as if he'd summoned it, was a *fox*, her golden fur glinting in the sunlight. Her black legs made it look as if she had walked through ashes, and her tail was balanced perfectly behind her. She stopped at the boy's feet and turned to face me.

"You have a pet fox?" I asked.

"No, no. She's not my pet. Wild animals can't be owned. Her mother was killed when she was a kit—baby foxes are called kits. I took her home and raised her till she was old enough to fend for herself."

"Why is she looking at me?"

"She keeps an eye out for danger. Maybe she thinks you're dangerous. Are you?"

I knew some people thought so, but I couldn't say that out loud, could I? After hesitating just long enough for the boy to look at me strangely, he said, "There's a lot of danger around here, you know. Changelings, of course. And all sorts of monsters. There are demons, and witches, and giants too. Giants are very danger-ous. Did you know there was a giant who killed a boy near here?"

"A giant *killed* a boy?"

"They were friends. It was an accident. Forgot his own strength as he reached out his hand to help the boy out of a boat. My father says the giant wept for seven years and died of a broken heart."

"That's not true."

"It is. You really can die of a broken heart."

"No, I mean the whole story."

"There's a church at the top of a mountain on an island not too far from here. They say the giant is buried underneath it. I'll take you—"

Just then, there was a loud sizzle and crack from the flames. The fox jumped back, circled an invisible spot a few times, and lay down in the grass. She carefully crossed her front paws, and the three of us turned together to watch the lightning-struck tree.

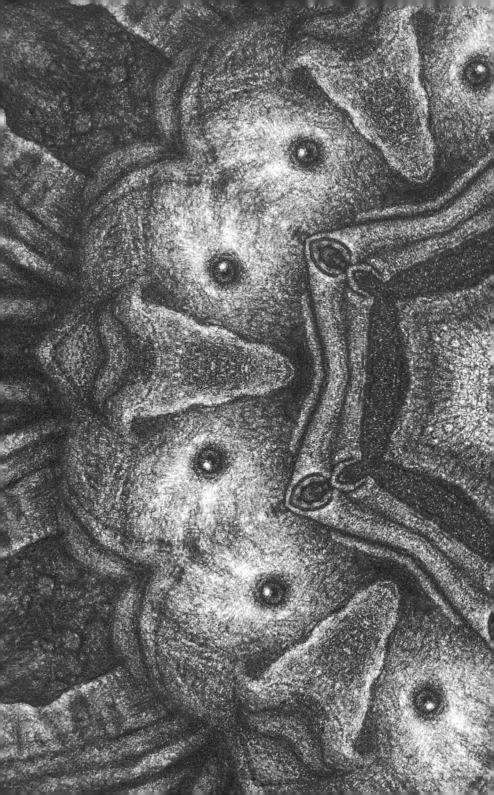

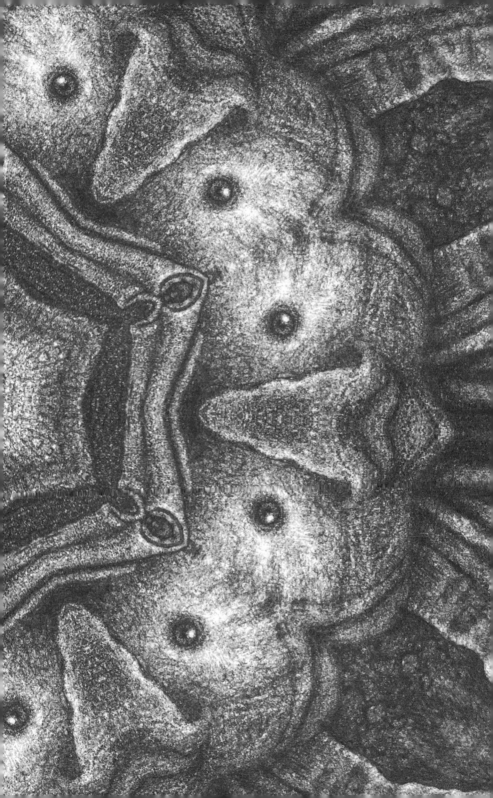

THE FUNERAL

·

F or as long as I could remember, James had sat next
to me at every meal. My mother made sure he had a
plate, a cup, and even some food. He came to school with
me, but he didn't have his own desk, so he stood behind
me or went off to play on the playground until the bell
rang and it was time to go back home. Sometimes in the
middle of the day we'd close the shades in my bedroom,
lie on our backs on the bed, and look at the glowing green
phosphorescent stars my mother had painted on my ceiling last summer. The three of us had watched on TV
as men landed on the moon somewhere high above us
all. James and I dreamed of going there one day, but for
now we pretended my bed was a rocket and we floated
through the private universe of my room. James and I
had the same dreams, and the same nightmares, and he
was the only one who understood all my fears.

I was getting older, and I know my mother worried
about James. She thought he should have disappeared
a long time ago, but he kept growing with me. When I
first met him, he was the little blue blanket my grandparents had bought for me. He was very soft and kept

me company and didn't talk, but that was fine because I didn't talk either. He didn't have a name back then, but I knew he was there, and when I began to speak, one of the first words I said was "James," which my mother did not understand.

James then had a series of transformations. He eventually moved out of the blanket and took up residence in my stuffed elephant. James remained the elephant for a while, and then one day I woke up and he'd become my left shoe. He didn't mind when I had to wear him, but my mother didn't like that I carried the shoe with me all around the house and into my bed. After a year he transformed into my mother's hairbrush, which really frustrated her because it was her favorite hairbrush. But James had to stay by my side, so the hairbrush left her dressing table and became mine. She got it back in time, though, because I heard him calling from the closet. When I opened it, I saw he'd become a broken black umbrella. I carried that umbrella around for several months, but it turned out his metamorphosis was not yet complete. One Saturday afternoon I picked up the umbrella and saw immediately it was just a regular umbrella again. "James?" I called out. "Where did you go?"

"I'm right here," came his voice.

I looked at all the objects in the room, but none of them were him. "I don't understand," I said. "What have you—"

And then I saw him. Well, that's not quite right. I *felt* him, standing right next to me. It was like he had finally emerged from his chrysalis, and was free.

After that, it was much easier for James to come to school with me, and I experienced a sense of freedom too. I no longer had to carry around strange objects from my house that made people ask questions. James was now able to follow me anywhere, and stand by me, and sleep beside me. But like I said, as I grew older, my mother continued to worry about our friendship. I heard her on the phone with a friend, wondering if she should take me to a doctor. Was it normal, she wondered, for a child my age to still have a friend like James? She was afraid that something was wrong with me, which she never said to me directly, and I grew angry. I felt betrayed by her, and I think that's why I didn't tell her when James died.

I don't know if he'd been dying for a while and I hadn't noticed, but the morning of my birthday, I woke up and James was gone. I knew in my heart he was dead, yet I still looked around for him, and wondered if he'd simply run away. Was it something I had done? Maybe he was just mad at me. It was as if I was trying to convince myself he couldn't really be dead. But he was, and I didn't know what to do.

My mother couldn't understand why I was so sad. I told her I had a stomachache, so I spent most of the day in bed. That night she brought two plates of cake, one for me and one for James. I burst into tears. I dreamed of James, and wondered what he would have looked like if he'd been real.

I knew what I had to do. While my mother was still at work, I snuck quietly around the house after school, opening closets and climbing up into the attic until I'd collected everything I needed. My arms full, I opened the back door and went outside. The air was cool and the moon was strangely visible, floating in the daytime sky. I found a spot in the forest that bordered my yard and began to dig. One by one, I buried my blue blanket, the stuffed elephant, the left shoe, my mother's hairbrush, and the umbrella. I covered everything with dirt and leaves and sat on my knees with my eyes closed. I said a prayer for James, and then I looked up at the early moon.

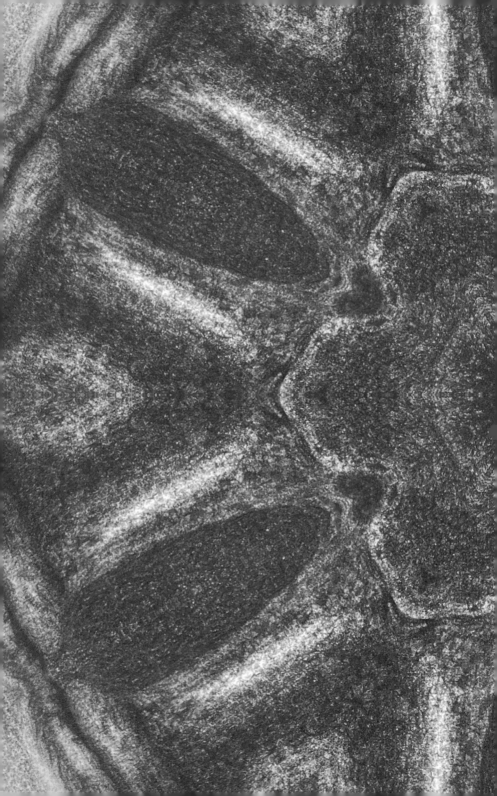

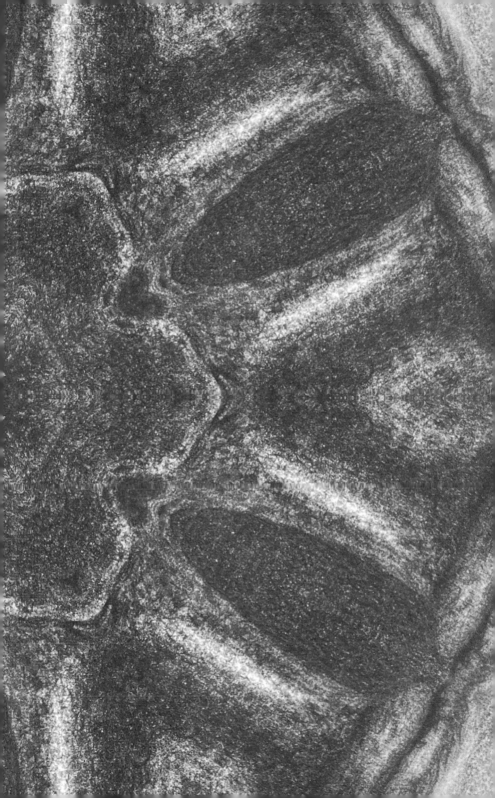

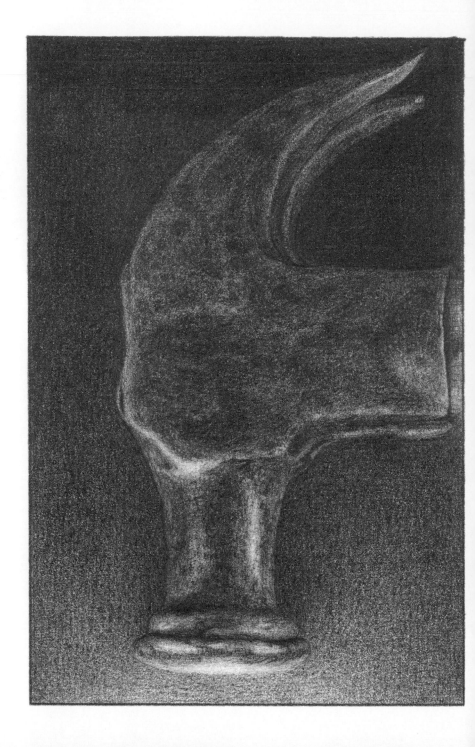

THE GLASS SHIPWRECK

•

J ames brought me to his grandparents' house only once, but I'll never forget it. They lived in Rahway, New Jersey. I can't remember what the occasion was, but their house was like a museum. All the furniture was encased in clear plastic, as if his grandparents were afraid the chairs and sofas were going to rot like fruit if they were exposed to the air. They had a life-size ceramic bulldog on the hearth of the fireplace that sometimes seemed to move, and above the piano was a large oil painting of a fortune-teller with bright green eyes, wearing a black lace shawl. Everything in the house smelled of butterscotch and talcum powder, except the sunroom, which was filled with plants and smelled like wet dirt and mushrooms.

There were thick sheets of glass on all the tables in the house, beneath which his grandparents had placed thousands of black-and-white photographs. It was as if their memories had to be kept from rotting too. There were probably an additional thousand pictures hanging on the walls. James pointed out a few he particularly liked: two framed images of Japanese kimonos created entirely from real butterfly wings, and a large silhouette of Abraham Lincoln in the hallway that was cut from black paper. He said he believed the president had actually sat for it during his lifetime.

There was one object James most wanted me to see. He brought me to it with a kind of hushed intensity, as if we were in a church and he wanted to show me something holy. There, hanging by the fireplace, was a small shadow box with a miniature three-dimensional scene inside it: a tiny ship made from black glass, sinking beneath blue sparkling waves. It was a bejeweled shipwreck, and the whole thing would have fit into the palm of my hand. At the same time we both reached out our hands and gently touched the edge of—

In a kingdom very far away, there lived a tormented man obsessed with catastrophes. He dreamed of volcanoes, fires, earthquakes, and floods. These apocalyptic visions filled his mind during the days as well, and his inner world was one of wreckage. He knew the world was filled with pain, and he could feel that pain burning in his brain, in his heart, and on the surface of his skin. To keep himself from going insane, he stole things he found beautiful. He was like a magpie, drawn to shiny objects, and soon he'd amassed a treasury of multicolored jewels. When he felt particularly tormented by the darkness, he'd hold his jewels up to the sun and try to become lost inside their dazzling colors. But somehow the beauty couldn't quiet his mind, and even though he knew it was irrational, he grew angry at the jewels themselves. He became hot all over and his mind went blank. When he came out of his fever, he discovered there was a hammer in his hand and his treasures had all been smashed into tiny bits.

Horrified at what he'd done, he swept up the ruins of his shining hoard and wept. Suddenly, he knew what he had to do. Using a magnifying lens and sharp tweezers, he built the catastrophes he saw in his head, piece by piece, inside wooden shadow boxes. Sometimes he'd spend months on end making orange flames from the shards of sapphires, and he'd create tiny trees from chips of emeralds and spun gold. He shaped flowing lava from splinters of rubies and carnelian, and he wove a tornado from silver threads and embedded it with diamond dust. But his favorite piece, the one he spent the most time sculpting, was a tiny ship he spun from black glass, sinking beneath an ocean of sapphire and topaz. When he finished the scenes, he placed small panes of glass on the front of the boxes, sealing each catastrophe inside. Every time he finished one of the dioramas, he hoped his nightmares would end, but they never stopped, so he kept working on the miniature scenes.

The man lived in an old house deep in the woods. He never spoke to anyone on the few occasions he went to town, and as the years passed, the townspeople noticed he stopped going altogether. Rumors spread that he had vanished or died, and one day a group of curious children found his abandoned house. They climbed through his broken windows and discovered his tiny catastrophes laid out on a table in the back. They didn't understand the value of the jewels the man had been using, but they loved the violence of the subject matter and how everything sparkled, so they stole the little boxes and brought them home. Some of the shadow boxes broke or disintegrated in their arms as they snuck them into their rooms that night, but a few were safely hidden in the backs of closets and drawers.

Over the next few decades, the rest of the little scenes were lost or destroyed, except for one. Wrapped in soft fabric and locked into a suitcase, the tiny delicate scene journeyed across land and sea. It was finally separated from its owner by an unfortunate accident in a train station, and the locked suitcase, now unopenable, was placed on a shelf in a vast room labeled "Lost and Found." There it sat, forgotten for years, until the time came for the station to be torn down and replaced by a shiny new one. The contents of the "Lost and Found" were sold off to the highest bidders. *The owner of an antique shop bought the unopenable suitcase along with two prosthetic arms, three ivory umbrellas, an elaborate wig, and other items you would never think people could leave behind in a train station.*

The owner of the antique shop happened to have a large box filled with tiny keys. When he had the time, he spent an afternoon trying them all in the lock on the suitcase and one of them finally, miraculously, worked. He discovered the glass shipwreck. His eyesight was failing him and he thought the entire thing was made from cheap glitter, so he put it up for sale in his shop for a few dollars. It was sold to a young couple who happened into the shop one day while they were on their honeymoon. They took it home and hung it on their wall by the fireplace, where it stayed untouched for the next forty years, until—

Suddenly, I opened my eyes. It was like I'd come out of a trance. James and I were no longer touching the glass shipwreck. He was staring at me and we were both crying. Neither of us said a word.

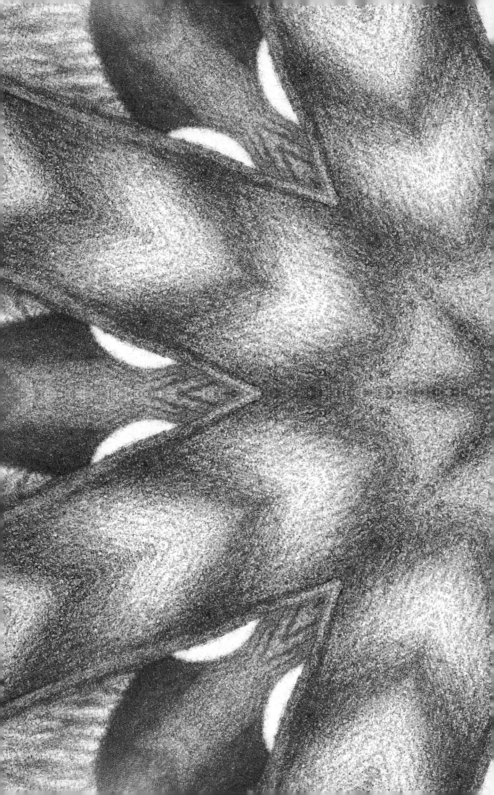

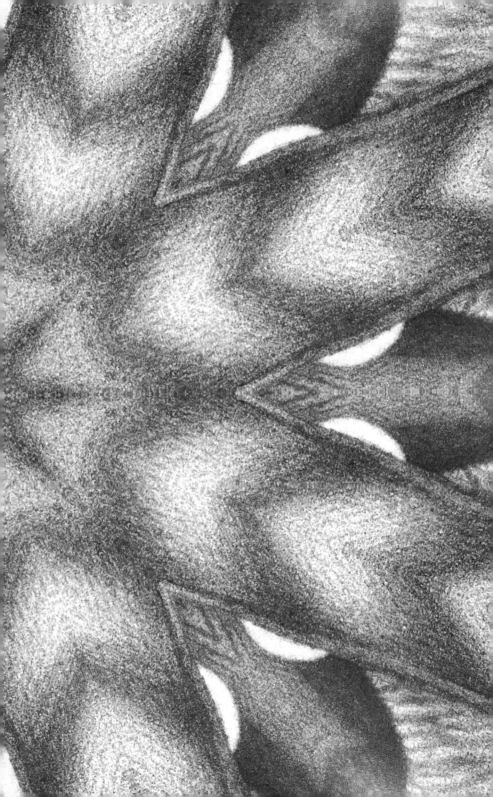

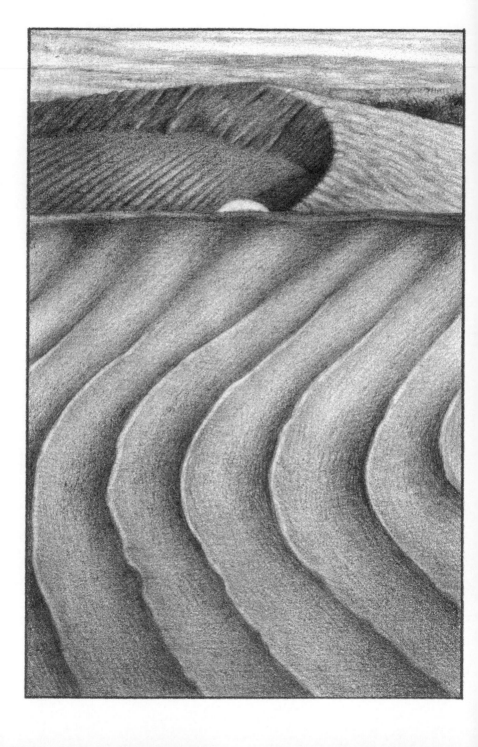

THE SPHINX

·

W e'd been walking through the dunes for a long time, and the sun was very strong. I'd rolled my sleeves up all the way and I was sweating a lot. The heat caused the air to ripple and I wondered if I'd made a mistake. Maybe it wasn't true. Maybe the Sphinx was not here and I shouldn't have listened to this boy I barely knew.

But then, over a rise in the sand, it appeared.

The Sphinx was taller than my house, and it stared toward us with the strangest expression, as if it was going to speak. I felt like I was face-to-face with time itself. The head sat high above its lion's body, the two front paws stretched out on the sand. I didn't know what to say, so I laughed out loud. Then James surprised me by grabbing my hand and pulling me toward the giant creature.

As usual, I'd seen James earlier that day at the local library after school. He was always there when I was there. We'd been in the same class since kindergarten but had never really spoken. I don't know why. He was a little strange and I guess I avoided him. Today, though, I was reading a book about birds. I had decided to learn the names of every bird on Earth—which is very hard, by the way, because there are so many types of birds.

I heard a voice. "Did you know the ancient Egyptians worshipped birds?" I looked up from my book. There was James standing in front of me, speaking as if we were in the middle of a conversation. "Or rather," he continued, "Egyptians worshipped gods with the *heads* of birds."

"Like Osiris and Horus," I said. I didn't want him to think I was unaware of the Egyptian gods.

He stared at me for a little too long, and I could see in his eyes he was trying to make some kind of decision. Finally, he said, "Do you want to see a Sphinx?"

"A Sphinx? Where?"

"In the dunes."

We lived in a small town in California at the edge of a desert with a famous wildlife refuge. By fifth grade, all the local children had gone for class trips. We hiked and learned about the plants, animals, and birds of the area. There was a lake, a boardwalk, a beach, and endless miles of sand.

"There are no Sphinxes in the dunes."

"There's one. It's from a movie."

"What are you talking about?"

"It was a silent movie. Two thousand people helped build a replica of an Egyptian city in the dunes. The entire thing was made from plywood and plaster. And when they finished filming it, the whole city was destroyed so no one else could film there. But one of the Sphinxes survived."

"How do you know this?"

"My uncle told me."

"I can't go to the dunes with you."

"Why not?"

"My parents would never let me."

"Don't tell them."

Two hours later, after a long bus ride and an exhausting walk through the sand, the Sphinx was looming over us. We wandered around its vast body. Much of the original plaster had fallen away, revealing a kind of wooden latticework, like the scaffolding that goes up around construction sites. We found an opening big enough to squeeze through and we stepped inside the Sphinx. The shade inside was cool and soft.

"You've been here before?" I asked.

"No," said James. "I didn't want to go alone."

We lay down inside the vast breezy expanse of the Sphinx's body. Side by side we looked up at the blue sky visible through the dissolving structure, and we talked about the Gods.

Part Three

EVENING

.

THE BOOK OF DREAMS

.

During recess, as all the other kids ran for the swings and tetherball courts, James knew where to find me. I always waited for him at the top of the three concrete steps leading up to the unused door at the back of the school.

"I invented something for you," said James with a smile as he sat beside me.

"Really?" I asked.

"Yes."

"What is it?"

"The Book of Dreams. It's a way to stop nightmares."

My nightmares had been getting worse, and James was one of the few people I'd told about them. I thought he was joking, so I laughed.

"I'm serious," he said.

I shouldn't have laughed. James was always inventing things. He kept a notebook filled with his ideas. We'd learned in art class about Leonardo da Vinci, who not only painted the *Mona Lisa* but also drew ideas for underwater vehicles and ways to fly, hundreds of years before the invention of submarines and helicopters.

I always imagined that James's notebooks were like Leonardo's, and in four hundred years, all his inventions would come true.

James opened his current notebook and tore out a piece of paper covered in writing and diagrams in blue ink. "I've been experimenting with it for a few weeks," he said, handing me the paper. "I think I've finally gotten it to work. Try it tonight and let me know what happens."

The bell soon rang, and we went back to our classes.

At bedtime, alone in my room, I carefully unfolded the piece of paper I'd kept in my pocket all day. Amid little sketches and arrows, James had written a set of directions for me to follow.

1. Look up at the ceiling when you are in bed.
2. Imagine the ceiling beginning to ripple like the surface of a lake.
3. Imagine a hole opening above you, like the end of a tunnel.
4. Imagine an angel coming down from inside the tunnel, holding a giant book. This is the Book of Dreams. It is filled with every dream in the world. Every dream is a good dream except for one chapter filled with

nightmares. You can see this chapter even when the book is closed, because the pages are black.

5. Reach up and open the book, but SKIP the chapter of nightmares.
6. Pick any dream you want.
7. The angel will then shut the book and take it back up, into the ceiling.
8. The hole in the ceiling will bubble over and close.
9. Go to sleep.
10. Have the good dream.

That night, for the first time in a long time, I had no nightmares. Instead, there were gardens, and an old house I loved, and someone's hand gently holding mine as we floated off to sea. Maybe it was just a coincidence, but I think James's invention worked. It's strange, but I can't remember if I ever thanked him. I hope I did, and I hope he was pleased.

I no longer have that piece of paper, and I don't need it to summon the Book of Dreams anymore, but I wish I had it.

I miss his handwriting, and I miss James.

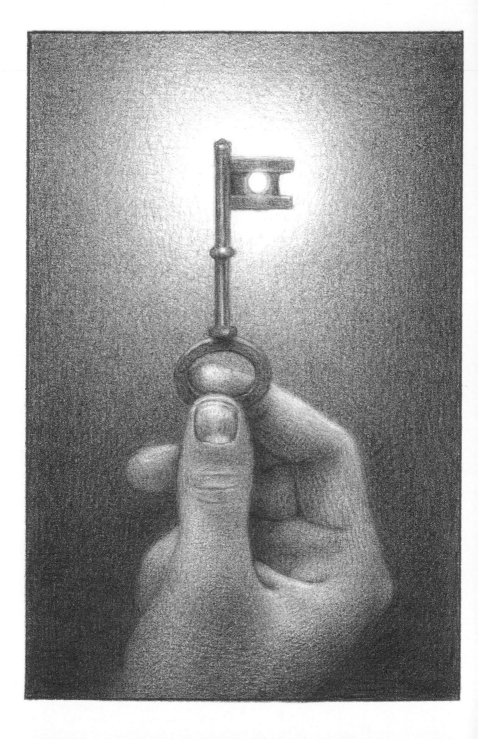

THE MYSTERIES

·

W e called our notebooks *The Mysteries*. We were up to *The Mysteries, Volume 7.* In these notebooks, mostly red spiral-bound ones we took from the supply closet at school, I wrote down the strange things that interested us. I wrote about ghosts, and reports of UFOs, and stories about monsters and witches and giants. James was a really good artist, so he drew the pictures.

We kept our notebooks beneath a loose floorboard in my room. James had an old silver key he liked to carry with him, so we pretended the key was needed to open the loose floorboard. On the nights that James slept over, we'd say good night to my mom, then we'd pull back my blue rug and he'd place his key in the imaginary lock in the air above the floorboards.

When we were finished, I'd return the notebook to its hiding place and James would lock it up with his key. Since the hiding place was in my room, I swore I'd never open it without his key, which meant I couldn't work on *The Mysteries* if James wasn't with me. That wasn't much of a problem because James slept over all the time, but one night, James reached into his pocket and the key was not there. He searched through everything, from his underwear to his pant legs and his shoes. He dug through his book bag and rechecked his pockets dozens of times, as if the key would suddenly, magically, reappear. The next day, we both went through our houses, practically turning everything upside down. We searched at school too, getting down on our hands and knees, saying we'd dropped our pencils, but the key was gone.

We returned to my room the next night and pulled up the blue rug. We stared at the floorboard. All we had to do was reach over and lift it up. The lock was not real. The key didn't actually do anything. Yet neither James nor I moved. We looked at each other but didn't say a word. It was the strangest sensation. What was stopping us? The lock and the key were just part of a game we played, but we'd both made a promise.

The notebooks stayed beneath the floor.

Later that year, after James died, my parents decided we should move. When everything in my room had been packed away, I finally rolled up my blue rug for the last time. In my mind I could still see the red covers of the notebooks beneath the floorboard, and I could still feel the joy of sitting beside James as I wrote and he drew. I wanted to hold those notebooks again because it would be like holding *him* again. I looked at the spot where the invisible lock was hovering in the air, and I still felt the power of James's lost key. I couldn't open the lock without it. But a voice in my mind that sounded very much like James said to me, "Open your hand." I hadn't realized my right hand was clenched in a fist. I uncurled my fingers. There, on my palm, was the key. It was as clear as day, and as invisible as the lock.

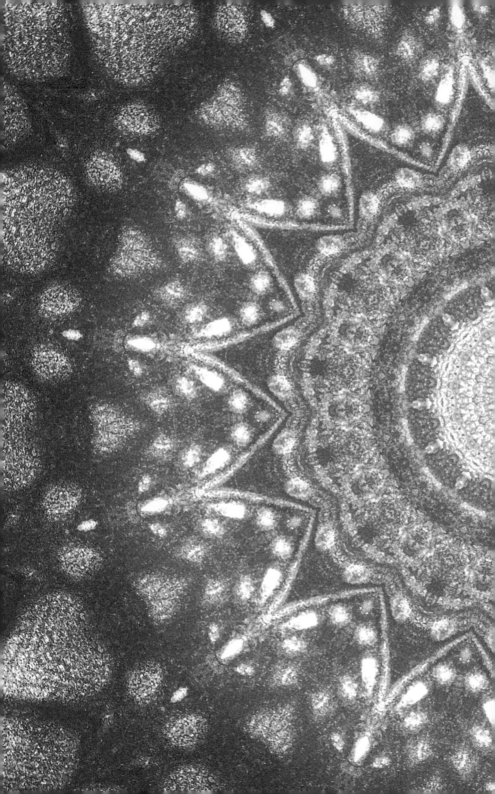

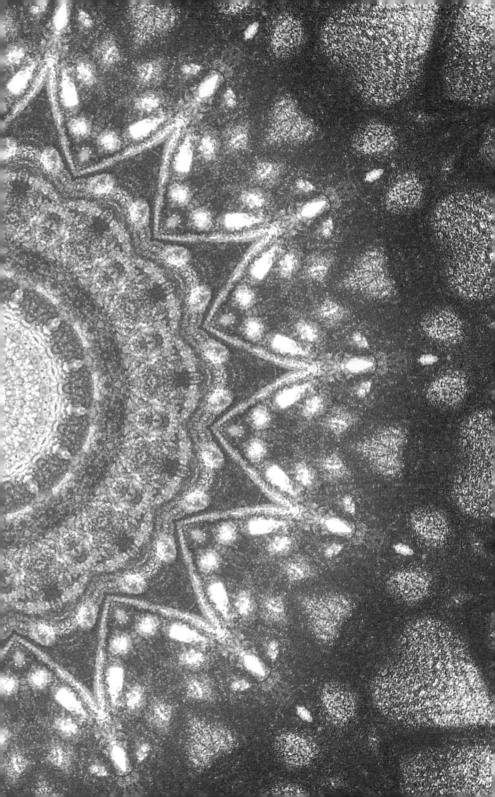

CHRYSALIS

•

James loved butterflies. He had read every book in the library about them. He wanted to memorize every kind of butterfly in the world, but he said there were 17,500 different species, so it was going to take him a long time.

One evening, when we were playing in my backyard, he spotted a chrysalis hanging from the underside of a yellow leaf. It was about the size of my thumb. His eyes lit up.

"Do you know what happens in there?" he asked me.

"A caterpillar turns into a butterfly," I answered.

"Yeah," said James, "but do you know *how* that happens?"

I pictured the caterpillar unzipping itself, like a costume, revealing the butterfly hidden inside its body. But I had a feeling that wasn't right.

"Tell me," I said.

"Well, the caterpillar attaches itself upside down to a leaf and sheds its skin like a snake, revealing the chrysalis inside. But the chrysalis is somehow *larger* than the caterpillar it comes out of."

"That's strange."

"But that's not the strangest part. The real mystery happens next. Scientists don't even really understand it."

"What happens?"

"Everything inside the chrysalis . . . dissolves."

"Dissolves?"

"Yeah, that's what's happening in there right now. Everything turns to liquid. It's like a magic potion. Inside it, little groups of cells called imaginal discs begin to grow, one for each part of the butterfly. They become the legs, the antennae, the wings. In the end, there's almost nothing left of the original caterpillar except its memories."

"That isn't true. A butterfly can't remember being a caterpillar."

"It can. Scientists have done studies. The butterfly remembers."

I thought about that for a moment. "So . . . maybe being in the chrysalis is like falling asleep and dreaming," I said.

"Maybe," said James, "except you completely come apart, and wake up in a new body with wings."

The chrysalis hung from the leaf like a jewel, and I closed my eyes. I found myself thinking about things that transform into other things. Tadpoles become frogs.

Frogs become princes. Princes become kings. I thought about seeds that become trees, which then become books and houses. I thought about clouds becoming rain, day becoming night, summer becoming fall, children becoming adults. And suddenly, in the cool, calm moonlight of my backyard, as a breeze moved gently through the branches and the air filled with the smell of lilacs and milkweed, it felt as if the entire world was becoming something new.

I don't know how much time had passed, but when I opened my eyes, it was too late. I was alone in the liquid night.

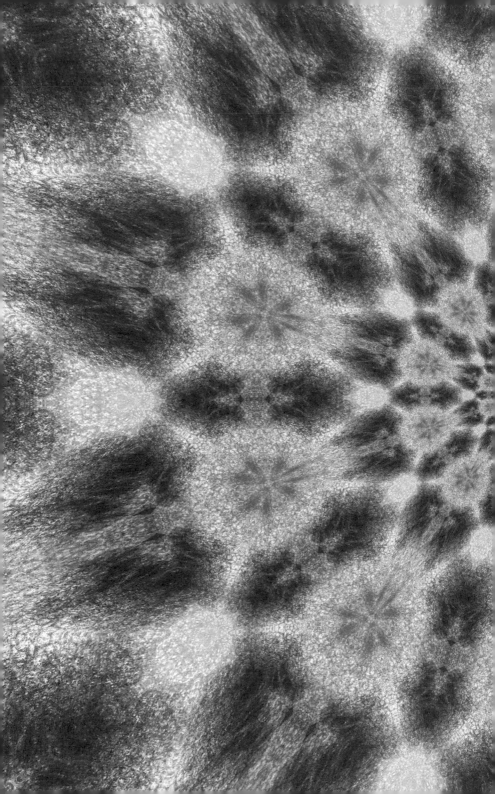

THE LIGHTS

•

I was new to town, so I spent a lot of time alone. I rode my bike down the unfamiliar streets, past all the little houses, and came to the elementary school. The building was closed. I rode up to the windows and looked inside. Most of the blinds were up and I could see into the classrooms, where all the desks were lined up in perfect rows. It was like a movie where all the people in the world had vanished mysteriously, and I was the last person left alive. I imagined rows of little ghosts haunting the school, wondering what had happened. I rode around to the back of the building, across the cracked blacktop where hopscotch games in yellow paint had faded in the sun. There was a small playground with a swing set, a tetherball court, and some seesaws. Behind them was the edge of a dark forest.

I rode across the lawn to the forest and saw a little path leading into the trees. I laid my bike on the grass and entered the woods. After I walked for a while, I came upon an arrangement of stones that caught my eye. Written on each stone was the fading name of what must have been a classroom pet. I imagined a long parade of grieving children walking to this spot, shoeboxes in hand, to bury in the ground the little friends they'd loved.

I lost track of time and didn't realize the sun was fading until it was too late. I could hear birds and insects in the air, and the leaves rustled all around me. I stood up, unsure which way to turn. I looked up and could see the outline of the treetops against the night sky. My mother had wanted me home before dark. She was going to be mad. I'd somehow gotten myself turned around and was no longer sure which way to walk. I couldn't see the path anymore, and the school could have been in any direction.

A shaft of light appeared through the trees. For a moment I thought it was the headlights of a car, but it was coming almost straight down, from above. It might have been an airplane, but there was no sound. In fact, I noticed that all the sounds of the forest had stopped and the air was completely still. The beam of light was slowly moving through the trees, as if it was searching for something.

Another beam of light soon appeared a little farther away, coming down from above. This light was red.

I squinted and looked up into the starry sky, visible between the black leaves above, and noticed lights that I thought for a moment might be stars, but they were bigger, and brighter, and they were moving. I was mesmerized even though what I was looking at made no sense. I wasn't scared, yet I found myself hiding behind a tree, my hands wrapped around the trunk. I looked into the forest again and now there were many beams of light, some red, some blue, some yellow, all moving slowly through the woods. Then, like a switch had been flipped, all the lights vanished. After a moment, the sounds of the insects and birds resumed. I stepped out from behind the tree. Everything looked and sounded so normal that I wondered if I'd been dreaming.

Then another light appeared, small and distant, flickering on and off. I was frozen in place as I watched it coming directly toward me, hovering a few feet off the ground. It seemed to know where I was, and I thought I had better run. I unfroze, turned, and quickly tripped over a root and fell face-first to the ground. Looking up, I watched as the light picked up speed. I opened my mouth to scream, but first I heard—

"You okay?"

Standing over me was the silhouette of a boy about my age on a bicycle. *My* bicycle.

"This yours?" The light on my handlebars sputtered and the batteries finally died. "I found it at the edge of the woods," he said as he put out his hand and helped me to stand. "I thought maybe you got lost."

I took my bike and followed the outline of the boy through the dark forest.

"You're new here," he said, our footsteps crunching in the leaves. "I know everyone in town."

"I just moved here with my mom."

"Have you seen them before?"

"Seen *what* before?" I asked.

"You know what I'm talking about."

"What *was* that?" I whispered.

"Everyone has a different opinion on that."

"It happens a lot?"

"Old people remember the lights from when they were kids, and they say their grandparents remembered them too."

"Is it from outer space?"

The boy shrugged in a familiar way that made me sad. "Might be Martians," he said. "Some say it's angels."

"Angels?"

"The religious ones say that. The pastor, of course, and a lot of the old people at church think it's angels. The scientific ones think it's a natural phenomenon, like the aurora borealis. They always threaten to call in some real scientists, but they never do."

"What do *you* think the lights are?" I asked.

The boy paused for a moment. "Sometimes I think they're angels. And sometimes I think they're Martians. And sometimes I think they *are* some kind of natural phenomenon, but . . ."

"But what?

"Mostly, I just think they're beautiful."

We continued on through the dark forest in silence. After a few minutes I could see a blue field of grass beyond the edge of the woods. If I hadn't known better, I might have mistaken the grass for a misty sea. I was afraid if I looked away, the watery illusion would be broken, and I wasn't sure I'd be able to explain to the boy what I was seeing.

At that moment, a vast expanse of rainbow-colored lights burst down from above. For as far as we could see, it looked as if the entire world had turned into jewels. The boy backed into me as we shielded our eyes. I thought I heard him call my name, but I knew that had to be impossible because I hadn't told him what my name was. I heard my name again and the voice seemed so familiar.

"James . . ." I whispered to the lights. "Is that you?"

I don't know when the boy had grabbed my hand, but I suddenly became aware of the tightness of his grip, and the lights washed over us like the sea.

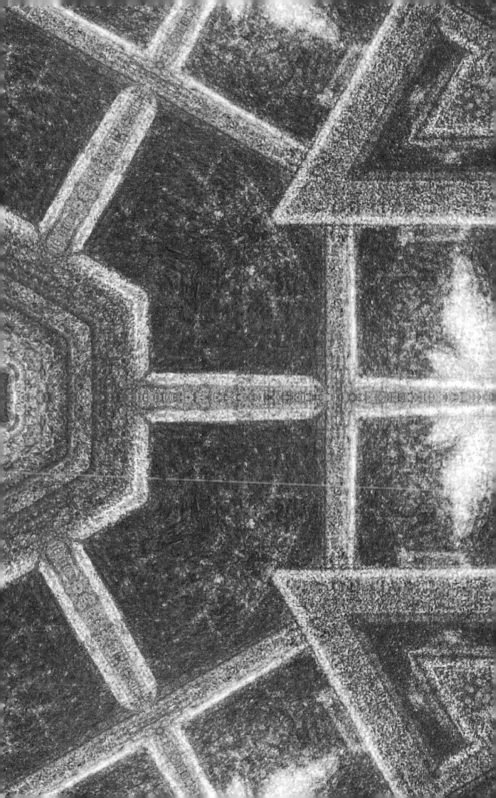

IN THE DARK

·

I woke up in the middle of the night after having heard a strange noise. I stumbled downstairs still wrapped in my blanket, but the house seemed to be empty. Then, in the darkness, came a voice.

"I've been waiting for you," it said.

I jumped with fright and looked around, but couldn't see anything. "Who's there?" I said. "What do you want?"

"I have something to tell you."

I reached for the lamp.

"Don't do that," said the voice.

"Why?"

"I don't like the light."

I was terrified, and I couldn't stand the dark. My heart was beating hard. I wanted the lights on so I could see who I was talking to. I reached my arm out and turned on the lamp. The light flooded the room like lightning for one brief moment, before something threw the lamp across the room, plunging us back into darkness. And then whatever it was came toward me as well. It felt as if I'd been hit by a train. Something big seemed to be on me, wrestling me powerfully on the ground. I tried to shake it off, but I couldn't get ahold of it. I twisted and turned, but the fabric of my blanket was pulled across my face and I couldn't see a thing. There was some kind of terrifying noise that seemed to be coming from all around me. I kicked my legs and flailed my arms, but I was facedown against the carpet, overpowered by whatever giant thing was fighting me. The harder I struggled, the bigger the thing seemed to become, and this went on for what felt like hours, until I was exhausted and realized there was no use fighting anymore.

As soon as I stopped struggling, the heavy thing released itself and let me go. In shock and out of breath, I sat up and pushed myself back against a wall. The blanket fell from my eyes and I saw the first blush of dawn was starting to move across the sky. My whole body ached. My eyes slowly adjusted and I looked all around me, trying to find the giant thing that had been wrestling me all night. But in the growing pink light of the dawn, the room looked just as it always did. Even the lamp was back in place.

"Where did you go?" I yelled. "Show yourself!"

"I'm right here," came the voice.

After a few moments I saw the tiniest bit of movement by the window.

I squinted.

Something shifted.

I rubbed my eyes.

Perched on the open window, no bigger than the palm of my hand, was a tiny black bat. He adjusted himself and turned to briefly look at the rising sun.

"That was *you?*" I asked in disbelief.

"Who did you *think* it was?" replied the bat.

"I don't understand."

"I told you not to turn on the light."

I stood up and brushed myself off. I moved cautiously toward the window. The bat's little feet moved impatiently on the window. I could tell he was eager to leave before the sun rose much higher in the sky.

"Wait," I said.

"What?" asked the bat.

"Didn't you have something you wanted to tell me?"

"Yes, I've been trying *all night* to tell you," said the bat. "But you wouldn't stop fighting me. It was very annoying. And now I have to go."

A sudden, strange kind of shame came over me. "I'm sorry," I said. "What were you trying to tell me?"

The little creature stretched his spiky wings. His eyes sparkled. "I've been trying to tell you I *love* you," he said, and with a little leap he vanished into the purple Connecticut sky.

THE GARDEN

·

The dragon was sitting in the branches of a dark tree. His emerald body blended into the leaves, making him almost completely invisible in the moonlight, but something shivered and he snapped into focus. Once I saw him, I couldn't unsee him.

"Come to me," he said.

"Why?" I asked. I'd never met a dragon before, so I was not afraid, but his teeth were sharp like tigers' teeth, and they shined among the green leaves.

"I want to whisper in your ear," he answered.

"No, thank you. I can hear very well from here," I said.

He narrowed his eyes. "Whose garden do you think this is?" he asked. It seemed like a trick question.

"James and I found it, so it's ours," I said.

"It is not your garden," said the dragon.

"Who are you talking to?" James, who was in the bushes chasing fireflies, asked.

"A dragon," I told him.

James emerged from the bushes and looked around.

"I don't see a dragon," he said.

"He's up *there*." I pointed into the canopy of the tree.

"I still don't see anything."

"Well, he's right there. He says this isn't our garden."

"Whose is it?" James asked.

"It's mine," answered the dragon in the tree.

"He says it's his," I told James.

"We found it fair and square," said James. "No one's been here for years. It's wild and overgrown. We're the ones who cleared the paths and pulled out the weeds. It's ours."

"Tell your little friend to calm down," said the dragon.

"Why can't he see or hear you?" I asked.

The dragon lifted his shoulders in a shrug, which seemed oddly familiar to me, though I couldn't place why. "I didn't create the world, I just live in it," he said. "Who am I to explain why things are the way they are?"

James got bored with me and wandered back into the garden to look for a fox he'd seen earlier. The dragon reached out a claw and said, "Have an apple."

He shook the leaves of the tree, and a single red apple was revealed at the end of a branch just over my head. It was very pretty. I reached up and plucked it.

"Oh. One little thing," he said.

"What?"

"About the apple."

"Yeah?"

"I've heard that if you take a bite . . ."

"What?"

"Well, there's a rumor. If you take a bite . . . afterward, you'll know everything in the universe."

I held the apple in front of me and noticed the way the moonlight glinted off its glossy surface, which looked as hard as rubies. "How would that happen?"

The dragon shrugged again. "How should I know?"

"You make it sound like a bad thing, to know everything in the universe."

The dragon raised its eyebrows. "I don't think it's good or bad."

"You do," I said. "You think it's bad."

"What do *you* think?"

"It would make school easier."

"You would never fail a test again, that's true," he said. "But it's not just facts."

"What do you mean? What else *is* there?"

"Oh, there's so much more. There are secrets, and illnesses, and horrors you can't imagine. There are stories and myths and lies and dreams. There are civilizations being born and people you love dying. There's everything to come, and everything that's ever been. All that could be yours."

"It's impossible to know everything in the universe," I said after a moment.

"Is it?"

"Wouldn't that make me like . . . God?"

The dragon smiled. "Aren't you the clever one?" he said.

I looked at the reflection of myself in the surface of the apple.

"What are you waiting for?" asked the dragon.

"I'm thinking," I said. "If I knew *everything*, there would be no mysteries."

"I suppose that's right. No more mysteries for you."

"There would be no wonder."

"Perhaps not."

"There would just be . . . answers. You don't feel wonder at things you know the answers to."

"I guess not," said the dragon.

"Life without wonder seems sad."

The dragon shifted in the branches. "Do you think God is sad?" he asked.

"I don't know."

A shiver went down my back, though I wasn't sure why. I looked around for James but didn't see him.

"James?" I called out. "Where are you?"

There was no answer. The night grew darker.

I looked up at the dragon. "Where did he go?"

The dragon shrugged again, and I realized why the shrug seemed so familiar. James shrugged the same way.

"Maybe he's gone," said the dragon.

"He was just here two seconds ago."

"Time is funny in the garden," said the dragon. "It speeds up and slows down in the strangest ways."

"James!" I called, louder now. I felt hot, like I was standing near a fire. The garden was quiet. I tried to remember exactly how long it had been since I'd last seen James. I had no idea. Everything seemed different somehow, except for the dragon, who seemed as if he'd been there forever. "Please," I said. "Where is James? What happened to him?"

"Find out," said the dragon, nodding toward the apple in my hand. "Go ahead. Take a bite."

A MEMORY

·

The mechanism to open the heavy curtains in our school auditorium had broken long ago, so the fluorescent lights were always on. Because of this, no matter how bright the sun might be shining outside, it always felt like nighttime inside the auditorium. Making it even more confusing, the hands on the clock in the auditorium had fallen off, so time never seemed to pass at all.

We had all been called for a surprise assembly, and everyone was excited because that meant we would miss some of our classes. The longer it took the teachers to quiet us down, the less we'd have to learn or memorize that day.

Sometimes assemblies were called so the principal could announce schoolwide field trips or awards. I used to love the auditorium because it was the room where James and I did school plays (with the curious thrill that went along with *actually* being in the school at night), but mostly it was because this was where he and I snuck away during the day to hide among the empty rows of chairs. In the timeless room, we'd listen to the footsteps passing outside in the hallway, and dream of things to come. It was the place where we first held hands.

I'd met James in first grade, though I don't remember how. He was smarter than me, and braver, but somehow we needed each other. He could keep secrets, and so could I. We'd read together at night during sleepovers. We were always building miniature objects to fill our secret worlds. Our masterpiece was a city made from twigs we'd built in the woods behind my house, with bridges and towers, lakes and telephone wires. There was even a graveyard made from tiny stones, like the larger ones I'd painted for our classroom pets when they'd died. The city lasted for months, getting bigger and more elaborate, until the hurricane came. We made detailed plans to travel across the ocean one day. He wanted to go to Egypt. I wanted to go wherever he wanted to go.

Around me in the auditorium, all the students' voices buzzed and hummed like insects. My parents had thought I should stay home from school today, but I needed to come. I alone knew why we had been gathered that morning. I alone was aware that in a few minutes the principal would quiet us down and then take a strange pause that would alert all of the two hundred and thirty-six other students that something was very wrong.

I don't remember leaving the assembly. I suppose no one saw me, and I wasn't stopped, and no one came to get me. I must have walked out to the front of the school, because the next thing I remember, I was watching a sweaty young man in a white T-shirt, his sleeves rolled up to the top of his damp arms, delivering a young tree from the back of a truck. Its roots were wrapped in a burlap ball. I heard the school secretary telling the man that the tree was to be planted in memory of a student who had just died. How they arranged it so quickly, I never found out.

The tree was small for a tree, but it was probably twice the size of James. I watched as it was placed in the hole in the ground. The young man with the rolled-up sleeves shoveled dirt around the roots until it stood firmly on its own. I imagined the roots unfurling and spreading through what was left of the burlap, growing outward into the soil, taking hold in the earth like arms. At the same time, above the surface, the tree was growing upward and outward, swirling and vibrating until it was a hundred feet tall, with a wide canopy of joyous leaves that covered much of the front yard of the school in shade for children still unborn.

James's parents quickly moved away. Their house remained unsold for a long time and it soon fell into disrepair. The windows were boarded up with plywood and the lawn became overgrown. Soon, everyone said the place was haunted. Stories began circulating through town that someone could be seen in a window at night, when the moon was full. I didn't believe any of that, but I still avoided passing the house when I walked to school. A group of boys who never knew James broke into the house one night and set it on fire. I remember watching the house burn against the darkness. It was the strangest feeling, like James himself was splintering, fragmenting, dissolving. He was everywhere around me, just out of reach. The sparks rose up into the sky and paused midair until there were moments when I couldn't tell the difference between the burning embers and the stars. But the embers always fell back to earth, or went out, while the stars remained undimmed.

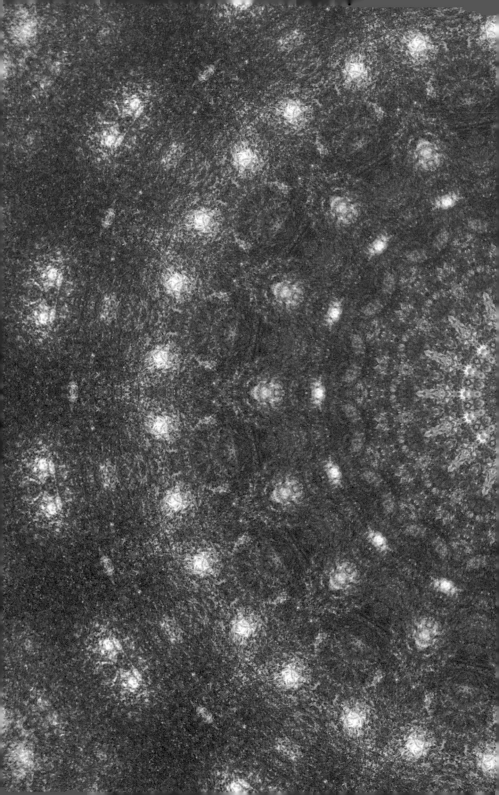

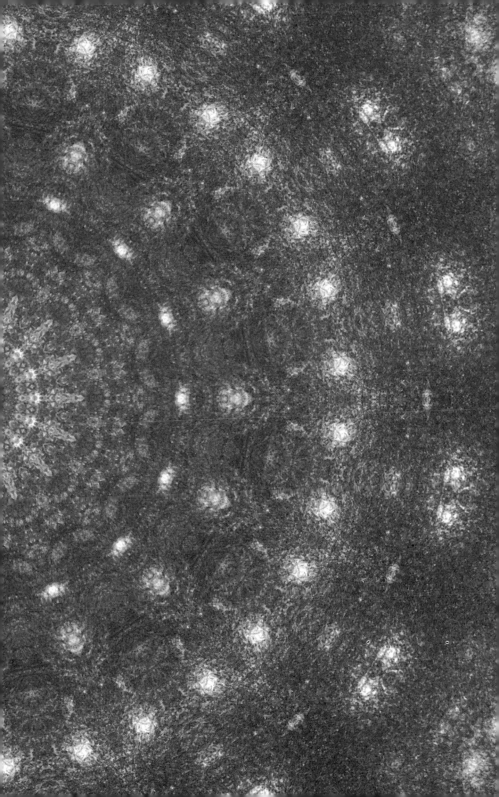

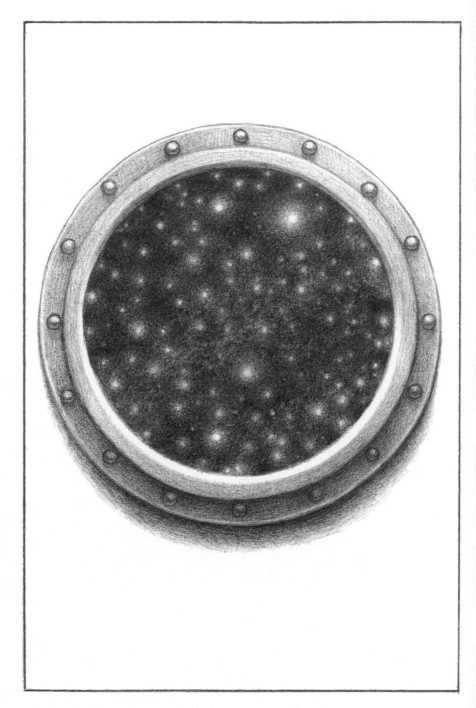

THE MIND OF GOD

•

I miss the Earth. It's hard to say how long we've been away, because it is very difficult to keep track of time when there are no real days or nights. We have lights that simulate the golden-yellow rays of the sun, and portals through which we can see the stars, but time doesn't really work out here. On Earth, the clock commanded our lives. I was always aware of the time, and the day of the week, and the month and year. I had made so many plans, mostly with James. *See you at my house at five,* I would write him, or *Meet me in the garden tomorrow after school.* There were mornings, afternoons, and evenings, and there were rainstorms and blizzards and heat waves. There was war and famine and flooding. But out here, none of that seems real anymore. Even James barely seems real anymore.

The expedition I am on will take many generations to complete. We are like migrating butterflies. There will be babies born on this ship who will never know the beginning of the journey, or the end. Their great-great-great-grandchildren will hear stories about our early years, and in the library, they'll read books about the

Earth, but life on a blue planet will sound to them like a fairy tale. They will be children of the universe, born in some unimaginable future in which I am nothing but a story.

Sometimes, when I am alone in my little silver room, I look out into the endlessness of space through my portal and read the books James gave me. I don't feel very much older than when we left, but at the speed we are traveling, I am aware that James has long since turned to dust. I picture the dust flying into the air, and some of it catching a ride into space, and it's almost like he is here.

In bed as I close my eyes, I wonder if the beginning of time and the end of time are the same thing, and the distance between seconds is really as long as the distance between stars. Maybe this is what it's like to be inside the mind of God. The past and the future mean nothing, and the time is always now.

AUTHOR'S NOTE

During the first three months of the pandemic, I was alone in my apartment in New York while my husband was stuck in California. During that time, I started making abstract art, perhaps because it felt like the world was shattering, so my art needed to do something similar.

For the previous five years, I'd been working on and off on a book, but when I finally was ready to think about the story again, I found myself ripping apart everything I'd already written. It was like the narrative was shattering along with everything else, and out of the shards a new book began to take shape. As I worked, certain themes and images kept reappearing: gardens and butterflies, apples, angels, fires, trees, friendship, islands, keys, shipwrecks, grief, and love. That's why I decided to call this new version of the book *Kaleidoscope*, because each of these elements, like bits of colored glass, turn and transform and rearrange themselves into something new. And like looking into a kaleidoscope, the view is always changing and only you can see it.

One of the constants in my mind as I wrote the story, though, was a house I know and love called Port Eliot, in Cornwall, England. My friend Cathy St. Germans lived there for many years with her husband, the late Perry St. Germans, whose family has owned the house for for more than four hundred and fifty years. Anyone familiar with Port Eliot will recognize the gardens, tunnels, hallways, doors, and windows of the beloved house in Cornwall. Cathy and Perry ran an arts and music festival on the grounds of their house, and it was at the Port Eliot Festival that this story began five years ago. I'd like to thank Cathy and Perry for that festival, but mostly for their friendship, which changed my life in so many ways.

I'd like to thank Lily Williams, whose father, Heathcote Williams, lived at Port Eliot with Perry from 1981 to 1991. Lily shared with me incredible memories about visiting the house when she was a child.

I want to thank my editor, David Levithan, for taking my hand in the darkness and helping me find my way through these stories.

My gratitude, as ever, goes out to Ellie Berger, Rachel Coun, Billy DiMichele, Charles Kreloff, Tracy Mack, Charisse Meloto, David Saylor, Lizette Serrano, and everyone at Scholastic who publishes my books with such love and care.

For their insights, conversations, help with research,

and inspirations, I'd like to thank Atlas Obscura (atlasobscura.com), Derek Brown, Jeanne Heifitz, Brandon Hodge at Mysterious Planchette (mysterious planchette.com), Tony Howard, Connor Jessup, Anna Reynolds, Connie Rock-man, Pam Muñoz Ryan, Holly Selznick, Lynn Selznick, and Brennan Spector.

And as ever, there would be nothing without my husband, David Serlin.

ABOUT THE AUTHOR

BRIAN SELZNICK is the author and illustrator of many books for children, including *The Invention of Hugo Cabret*, which won the Caldecott Medal and was made into the Oscar-winning movie *Hugo*, directed by Martin Scorsese. His other books include *Wonderstruck* and *The Marvels*, as well as *The Dinosaurs of Waterhouse Hawkins*, written by Barbara Kerley, which won a Caldecott Honor; *Amelia and Eleanor Go For a Ride*; *When Marian Sang* and *Riding Freedom* by Pam Muñoz Ryan; and the Doll People trilogy by Ann M. Martin and Laura Godwin. He collaborated with his husband, David Serlin, on the beginning reader, *Baby Monkey, Private Eye*, and illustrated a book for adults with poems by Walt Whitman called *Live Oak, with Moss*. He wrote the story for Christopher Wheeldon's production of *The Nutcracker* at the Joffrey Ballet and illustrated new covers for the twentieth anniversary of the Harry Potter series. He and his husband live in Brooklyn, New York, and San Diego, California. Visit him at thebrianselznick.com.